Without a word, Alex turned and rested her head against his chest, and his arms closed around her.

"I'm Hunter," he said softly.

"Alexandria Lord-Wright Foster," she said, smelling him and the rain and the green grass.

With his chin atop her head, his arms around her back, she felt completely safe. Alex looked up at him, and he smiled a little. Her heart thumped strong, steady beats.

"That's a big name for such little shoulders," he said.

"I make it work." *Even when I don't want to.*

With his thumb, he eased water from her cheeks. Alex didn't know if he distinguished her tears from rain, but she wasn't going to tell him she'd been crying. Lord-Wrights didn't cry in public, if at all.

CARMEN GREEN

was born in Buffalo, New York, and had plans to study law before becoming a published author. While raising her three children, she wrote her first book on legal pads and transcribed it onto a computer on weekends before selling her first novel in 1993. Since that time she has sold more than twenty-six novels and novellas, and is proud that one of her books was made into a TV movie in 2001, in which she had a cameo role.

In addition to writing full-time, Carmen is a busy mom, a full-time student completing her master's degree in creative writing, and teaches writing at a local school one evening a week. She's a founding member of the Femme Fantastik Tour, a group of writers who tour military bases promoting their literary works throughout the United States and Europe, and a volunteer in her community. In her spare time Carmen likes going to concerts, gardening, vacations in quiet, tropical places and going on long cruises that don't require her to do anything but read, sleep and eat.

CARMEN GREEN

THIS TIME FOR GOOD

KIMANI™
ROMANCE

KIMANI PRESS™

ISBN-13: 978-0-373-86065-4
ISBN-10:   0-373-86065-X

THIS TIME FOR GOOD

Hello Harlequin Readers!

I'm so excited that *This Time for Good* is my first book with Harlequin! I've been a writer for more than 15 years and have been a big fan of Harlequin authors, so I'm excited to be able to share my work with you too.

This Time for Good is part of a trilogy called the THE THREE MRS. FOSTERS, which I'm writing with fabulous author friends Brenda Jackson and Carla Fredd.

Marc Foster was a bad boy who thought he could get away with marrying three women, but he didn't count on the determination, fortitude and intelligence of his wives, Alexandria, Danielle and Renee.

It's true that love will cure what ails you, and it takes the love of three special men for the women to overcome the destruction of Marc's deception.

I'd love to hear from you, so visit my blog and leave me messages at www.carmengreen.blogspot.com.

Blessings,

Carmen Green

Your love and support sustained me through it all.

Tracy Cardwell, Pam Roach, Cherrita McCray, Giselle Williams, Glendora McCray, Kristen Suto, Martha Carter, Joyce Wilson, Denise Wilson, Janatune Alwakeel, Madeenah Dawson-Alwakeel. Tim Cardwell. Harold Cardwell. Dad. The Sparrow.

Love,

Carmen

Chapter 1

Alexandria knew her father didn't think she was a genius, but she wasn't dumb, either.

"Daddy, shouting isn't going to convince me to give you controlling interest in Wright Enterprises. Now, will you please sit down? Your blood pressure is probably off the charts."

Feeling as if she didn't have a friend in the world, Alexandria Lord Wright-Foster forced herself to stop fidgeting.

Her father had chosen to fight for his mother's money in a court of law instead of visiting her in the final months of her life.

Because of that decision, Grandma Letty had left all of her money, and shares of the company stock, to her only frequent visitor, her newly-wed, twenty-three-year-old, college dropout, never-been-in-charge-of-anything-but-decorating-the-conference-room granddaughter, Alexandria.

Her father may have lost the fight, but he was still angling to win the war.

"My blood pressure will be just fine when things start to run like they're supposed to around here. I've got some papers for you to sign." He tried to persuade Alexandria with a tone that said he'd take the deal if it were offered to him. "You'll get market value for the stock, and then you can go back to spoiling yourself."

"Daddy, I've already told you, those days are over."

"So, no more trips to New York for purses and shoes?" he challenged. "No more spa weeks in Arizona? No more couture fashion shows in Paris?"

"Ever since Marc and I got married, I've taken the family business seriously. I've been here every day learning this business and pulling my weight. I don't shop like I used to, and I don't party like I used to. I've changed. I'm a businesswoman."

"You can't play at this. You have no business skills and no business background."

"Daddy, you don't have a degree, either, and neither did Grandma Letty, and she was quite successful. So I've learned the same way you and she learned—on the job."

A tiny sound of disbelief left her father's mouth, but that was all.

"The bottom line is that I won't sign my stock over to you. Would you like something to drink? I'm having mineral water. Jerry? Mervyn," she asked her brothers who hadn't said a word through the entire exchange. "Would you like a glass?"

Jerry shook his head. He was the youngest brother, but older than Alexandria by ten months, had walked in late and sat at the head of the table, and nobody had corrected him.

Symbolically, that seat had been left empty after Big Daddy, their granddaddy, had died two years ago.

Jerry didn't know about the unspoken rule, having just returned from living in Texas. A concussion had ended his pro football career, but he was trying to get into the swing of things. He was very quiet and only answered questions when spoken to directly.

Marc, her husband, liked Jerry best.

Beneath the table, Alex pushed Send on her BlackBerry, hoping Marc would pick up.

For the past month he'd been in Philadelphia, but he'd been helping her practice assertiveness by webcam. Over a year ago he'd bought the book *A Fool's Guide to Being Assertive.*

Initially, she'd been offended. But once Marc had explained the book, then read it to her, then torn off the cover and made love to her to make up for offending her, she'd liked it. That's why she'd initially fallen in love with him. He'd helped her realize that although she didn't have degrees, she was smart, and the world needed people like her.

"You're costing us money, honey."

"How, Daddy?" she asked.

"All this waffling." He laughed in that big way corporate men did when nothing was funny. "You're offering refreshments and we're trying to discuss business."

Alexandria lowered her glass of water and wiped her lip with the cloth napkin.

Her BlackBerry vibrated and she glanced at it then sent the call to voice mail. The same number had called four times, but it wasn't Marc. She'd answer if they called again. Maybe he'd lost his phone and had to get a new one.

"We don't have time for you to schedule your mani-pedi," her brother Mervyn added, their father's living puppet.

"I know, Mervyn. This is what I came to say. Too much money is going out of the company."

"You have to spend money to make money," their father interrupted, as if everyone knew that but her. "If you'd gotten your college degree like your brother here, you'd know that. But I'm not holding that against you. You're a helluva decorator."

Alexandria's face heated under the sting of his sexist sarcasm. She wanted to be immune to their bullying, but she wasn't. She bit her lip and her father's eyes lit up like the lights on a pinball machine. He knew he'd hurt her.

"That's what I'm talking about, little girl. You're out of your league. You need to be home with your husband. How long has it been since he's been home?"

"A month," she said softly.

"Give that man some babies," Mervyn Jr., chimed in all his fatherly glory. "You're always here in Atlanta, he's always gone. That might go

a long way to helping Mama, in her delicate con-
dition."

The audacity of Mervyn's words made her
want to throw water on him. He'd done nothing
to help his kids to bond with their mother. Were
it not for their mothers, they wouldn't even know
they had a grandmother.

"Mervyn, you have five kids, a sixth on the
way. If Mama was going to shake her depression
because of children, she should be doing the
electric slide right now."

"Shut up, Alexandria. You don't belong here.
We've been doing just fine without you."

"Grandma Letty didn't agree with you,
Mervyn, or she'd have left you the money. But,
oh, right, you didn't go visit her either. So I guess
that means that I'm in charge. If you don't like it,
you can always get out. If you stay, *you* shut up."

Alexandria couldn't believe what had just come
out of her mouth, but she was proud of herself.

Then Mervyn started shouting.

"Enough!" her father roared.

She grabbed her briefcase and put it on the table.
"I don't need a degree to know that you're stealing
from us. We're not getting paid on certain accounts,
and that's bad business. It's all right here in this

report." She pushed the papers to the center of the table and Mervyn grabbed them and walked away.

"You—you had us audited?" he stammered, glaring at her over his shoulder.

"Yes, I did."

"When?"

Alexandria sat up straighter. "Yesterday. These are the first findings."

"How dare you?" he demanded. Their father tried to see the report, but Mervyn held it close to his chest.

"What does it say?" their father demanded.

"Nothing." Mervyn's rapid response was faster and louder than hers, and meant to deceive. His eyes seemed to be begging her not to reveal his secrets.

"You're stealing from the family." She spoke slowly so her father and Jerry could hear. "No more access to petty cash for you."

"Petty cash." Their father laughed in her face. Alex looked at Jerry and he shook his head.

"How much could it be? This is nonsense. You took a stranger's word over your brother's?" Mervyn Sr. asked his daughter.

"Not just someone. A certified public accountant, Daddy. A thousand dollars a week, sometimes more. He gets the money in cash from the office manager who logs it into a ledger."

"Excuse me." Willa, the receptionist, stood in the doorway. Tall and lean, she answered the phones beautifully, but had no self-esteem, thanks to a whorish ex-boyfriend who lived in the same building and whose bedroom wall adjoined Willa's. She could hear every headboard bang. Every night.

Alex had shared her assertiveness book with Willa last week. She was currently on chapter two. "I have an urgent call—"

Alex gave her a nod of encouragement.

"No interruptions!" Mervyn Sr. barked.

Willa stayed in the doorway, undecided. "Um," she said, brushing her bangs from her forehead.

"Get out!" her father roared.

"Willa—" Alex called, but the woman was already in motion. She ran down the hallway and through the door leading to the reception area.

She was probably in tears, packing her purse and getting ready to quit. Seven receptionists had quit the job since the previous March.

"Daddy, one day your outbursts are going to get you in big trouble. Everyone doesn't have to become accustomed to them like we have."

Alex picked up her BlackBerry and made a notation.

"What are you doing?" Mervyn demanded.

"Trying to keep the best receptionist we've ever had. I'm going to send Willa a fruit basket and a gift certificate for a mani-pedi. That will make her feel better."

"How dare you talk about me spending money, when you're ordering baskets and having independent auditors snoop into our family business. How dare you?"

Mervyn Jr.'s false indignation was almost funny in light of the trouble he was facing. "I dare because, before she died, Grandma Letty ordered this audit to be performed."

Jerry got up and walked slowly out the room and down the hall to check on Willa. They seemed to have formed an unlikely bond in the weeks since Jerry's return to Wright Enterprises. Willa taught him the phone system and he built up her broken self-esteem.

Alexandria showed her father and brothers the letter in her grandmother's handwriting. Their father sat down, unwilling to say a cross word against his mother.

"The first findings show that you've been embezzling for over five years at about sixty thousand dollars a year. You might have to go to jail."

Alex felt too vulnerable sitting down as her brother paced, but she didn't want to seem out of control either. She perched on the end of her chair.

Their father's chair bumped the table and he stood, looking alarmed. "That's a bunch of nonsense. I'll get my attorneys on these accountants and when they're finished, they'll wish they'd never set foot in this building."

Alexandria let her head fall back and she clasped her hands.

"Why are you praying?" Mervyn asked, his voice full of disdain.

"Because I was afraid the meeting was going to go this way. Daddy, do you want to see Mervyn behind bars? How will you explain to Mama that you let Mervyn steal from the company *and* then let him be thrown in jail?"

"What are you talking about? I'm not going anywhere," Mervyn said, his gaze shifting to their father to confirm.

Alex placed her hands on her folder. "If Daddy calls his attorney, we'll have to call the police. We will then file a report and explain the missing money for the past five years.

"The accountant said over three hundred thousand dollars has been illegally paid to you and not returned. Since you never made any attempt to pay it back, it's embezzlement. You will be arrested and jailed."

Her father glared at her brother. "Mervyn *borrowed* the money with the intention of paying it back."

Alex knew she had them where she needed them, but she made sure she looked as if she didn't believe her father's borrowing story. "Well, they said there might be a way."

"What way?" Mervyn Jr. asked.

"You can pay back the money today, and we can avoid calling the cops. Do you have cash, Mervyn?"

He stared at her in disbelief. "I don't have that kind of money."

Alex shook her head. "That's not good. Well, Daddy, there are two other ways. But you and Mervyn have to make a commitment. Why don't you sit down."

Her father practically growled. "What is it, Alexandria?"

"Well, we haven't been paid on twelve jobs, for a grand total of six million, five hundred fifteen thousand dollars and sixty-five cents. But if you could get those accounts paid up today, the accountants might be able to put Mervyn on a repayment plan and work something out."

Alex held her position, hoping they took her seriously, because she didn't know what else to do.

Her father nearly choked. "What?" He sifted through the papers again. "These people are my friends. I can't go asking them for money."

"That's what the report says. The accountant said that's the only way to go."

Mervyn Jr. avoided looking at the papers their father set in front of him.

Willa came back to the door. "I'm sorry, but there's an urgent call for Alex on one. And, Alex, there's a man in the lobby for you named Hunter Smith. He said it's important."

A chill skated down Alex's back and she stood, noting that Willa had her Louis Vuitton doggie bag on her shoulder. Where was she taking her Chihuahua, Little Sweetie?

"You're fired." Mervyn Sr. yelled at Willa, rising from his chair. "Get your things and get out of here. I haven't ever met a receptionist that can't follow simple instructions."

Willa nodded, tears rolling like a waterfall down her cheeks. "Alex. Please come here."

Outside the glass-enclosed conference room, Willa handed her a wireless handset for her to take the call in private.

"Is she deaf?" her father asked Mervyn so loud Alex could hear everything.

"Mervyn—" Alexandria opened the door and stuck her head in "—if you say anything ugly, I promise you're not going to like it. You don't have to be like Daddy."

Mervyn Jr. stood between Alex and their father. "Alex, you don't own me. She's not deaf. She's probably just as dumb as you are."

Alex took the doggie bag from Willa's arm. The poor girl was sobbing and Little Sweetie was trying to get out of the bag and lick at her tears.

"I hope you're happy," Alex told her brother, "because you're fired. And you're going to be under arrest."

"Oh, no, Alex," Willa objected, backing into the wall behind her. "I'll leave."

"No, you won't. It's time I stopped being intimidated by them."

"Fired?" Mervyn Jr. shouted. He stepped into a chair, trying to come across the conference-room table. "You need a man to show you your place."

Alex got the impression that her brother, who

was five years older than her, wasn't planning to have a reasonable discussion.

She grabbed her keys off the table and locked her father and brother inside the conference room. They could easily unlock the door, but that would slow him down.

"Go up front and call security," she said, eyeing Mervyn. She had never seen him so angry.

Well, he'd just lost his real job and his side income. He was facing arrest, and there was a current Mrs. Wright and two ex-wives with babies he needed to provide for. Mervyn would be uncomfortable for a long time.

Willa looked like a gazelle running to the lobby. She threw the door open and screamed, "Call security!"

Alexandria rolled her eyes. She could have done that.

Mervyn was still shouting from inside the glass walls of the conference room, but Alexandria blocked him out. Had she not left her purse inside, she'd have been on her way. Security was on their way up. Once she got her bag, she'd leave. Being the boss was hard work.

The handset Willa had given her beeped and she answered. "Hello?"

"This is Chris Foster. Marc's brother."

"Marc? My Marc?" Alex balanced on one heel while leaning forward to get away from the noise.

"Yes, your husband. My brother. Marc Jacob Foster."

"My husband doesn't have a brother. Excuse me a minute, please, Chris."

Her father and brother continued their loud argument as a man walked through the door with Willa.

He was tall and strong, muscles bulging from beneath the jacket of a well-made suit. He didn't look uncomfortable, just that he didn't want to be there. She agreed with him.

His dark eyes missed nothing. Not her brother behind the glass wall gesturing toward her. Not her father telling her how disappointed he was in her behavior and how she wasn't going to get away with anything. Not Willa, who sobbed as if she'd been shot, and Little Sweetie who was barking his head off.

Her entire family was an embarrassment.

This man had been in her life for forty-five seconds and she didn't like him. He'd seen her at her absolute worst and anybody that saw that was somebody she didn't want to know.

Instantly, her defenses went up. She didn't trust him. He didn't look as though he'd hurt her, but he looked as if he could if he wanted to.

"Who are you?" she asked him with a fake-patient smile in her voice.

"I'm Hunter. Are you ready to go?"

"And just where would I be going with you?"

"Have you talked to Chris Foster?"

"He's on the phone now."

"I'll be standing by when you're done."

He stepped back to give her privacy. Without understanding why, she appreciated that about him. The men in her life were without considera-tion and she always felt inferior, but not anymore.

"Okay." Alex heard her southern twang and took a few deep breaths. It was always more pronounced when she was stressed or after a long day. "Can you make yourself useful and hold this?"

She handed Hunter Smith her shoulder Vuitton doggie bag, turned and gestured inside. "My purse is inside. Can you get that without letting my daddy and brother out? Security is on the way to arrest my brother. It's a long story. He wants to hit me, so it's important that doesn't happen." She smiled and nodded her head. "Thank you."

Plugging her ears, she turned her back on the whole mess.

"I'm sorry, Chris. You caught me at a bad time. My husband didn't have any family. He was an orphan. You have the wrong number, and as I'm sure you can hear I'm kind of busy right now."

"Mrs. Foster, my brother wasn't truthful with you. I'm very much alive, and very much his brother."

"When was he born?" she asked him.

"May 5."

"That's right. What city?" she said quickly.

"Costa Woods, California."

"That's not true. He was born in Macon, Georgia."

"No, he wasn't. Marc Jacob Foster was born in Costa Woods, California."

"He has a birthmark—" she began.

"It's shaped like a boot of Texas on the inside of his right knee," Chris finished. "He has a scar on his shoulder from falling out of a tree when he was six years old trying to reach a cat that had climbed up and wouldn't come down. Seven stitches," they said together.

"That's right," she said slowly as the reality of his words hit home.

"Why would Marc say he didn't have a brother?"

"I can't answer that right now, Mrs. Foster. I've made all the funeral arrangements."

There was a loud crashing noise and Alexandria didn't even want to know what was going on behind her. This day had turned out to be a day she shouldn't have gotten out of the bed. But she knew that not looking at the mess didn't mean it wasn't going to be there. So she turned around.

Her brother had tried to pile chairs against the conference-room door to keep the police out, but they weren't amused.

He was on the floor being handcuffed while their father stood by dialing his phone. No doubt calling his attorney.

"It sounds like you're at the zoo."

"About the same thing. It was a board meeting," she said.

"Your husband, Marc Jacob Foster, my brother, born May 5, died in an airplane crash."

She braced her hand on the wall and all her gold bangle bracelets rattled. "Marc can't be dead," Alex broke in, keeping her voice steady despite the panic that shook her rib cage. "I talked to him two days ago, and he helped me…with something." Alex took the phone to the far end of the hallway and pressed herself into the corner.

"He's dead, Alexandria. I know it's hard to comprehend. But he's gone. I've made the arrangements," he said compassionately. "You're booked on Delta flight 1135 from Atlanta to Los Angeles. There's a layover before catching flight 231 to Del Rosa. Your seats are row 15A and 27B. A friend of mine, Hunter Smith, has agreed to be your escort so you won't be alone. I've known Hunter since my days in the bureau. He's a trustworthy guy who owns his own security company in Atlanta. The funeral is tomorrow here in Del Rosa, California. Do you have any questions?"

"Your friend is already here. Can I trust him? He's no rapist, is he?"

"No, ma'am."

"*Ma'am* is my mother. I'm Alexandria, or Alex. I have another question."

"Go ahead."

"Where are rows 15A and 27B? They don't sound like first-class unless there's a plane of all first-class seats. You know, I've never seen that before." Alex tried to block out the sound of her brother gurgling.

"They're not in first class."

"Oh." Her stomach bottomed out. She'd never sat in coach before.

"Where will Little Sweetie go?"

"Who's that?"

"My Chihuahua."

"Sorry. You'll have to leave him home."

"I don't travel without him."

Silence grew, but he broke before her. "I'll call Hunter with an update if changes can be made. In the meantime you have two hours to pack and get to Hartsfield-Jackson Airport. Hunter's a good man. He's really efficient."

"Yeah. He's kneeling on my brother's back now while the cops are cuffing him."

"What?"

"Nothing," she said, trying not to cry.

"Okay," Chris said, dragging out the word. "He'll escort you to your home to get your essentials and then bring you out here. See you tomorrow. Again, my sympathies."

Alex looked at the dead phone in her hand.

Hunter helped Mervyn to his feet and brushed him off.

Her heart squeezed in her chest. Her family couldn't know that Marc might be dead. They'd really steamroll her then.

She had to get out of there, but if her father saw her face he'd know something was wrong. Then she'd break down and ask her dad to help her find out if Marc was alive or not. Then she'd be a vulnerable needy girl again, instead of a woman in control of her life and able to run a company.

Heading down the hallway, Alex scooped up Little Sweetie's bag, grabbed her BlackBerry off the table, took Willa by the wrist and pushed her wayward group forward. Hunter followed with her purse on his arm.

"Where are you going?" her father demanded.

"I've said all I came to say. Now that Mervyn's fired and on his way to jail, I guess you're going to have your hands full. I'll be back in a few days. Daddy, you have to collect that money and turn it in or no new projects will be green-lighted. Willa, stop crying now." The woman's sobbing instantly became tiny hiccups.

"Very good. Daddy, new credit cards will be issued tomorrow. The accountant will have them."

"You will not leave here like this, Alexandria."

"Daddy, I have to go to California. Today. Now. I'm leaving. If you have a business expense, submit it to the accountants in grand-mother's office. Do not yell at them. They're not as nice as me. I'll call you in a few days. Thanks. Bye, y'all."

"In three days, this company will be back to the way it's supposed to be."

"Okay, Daddy." Alexandria met her father's gaze evenly. "We'll see."

He got in the elevator and rode down, no doubt to save his son.

Dragging Willa behind her, Alex held on to Little Sweetie's doggie bag and shushed him. He ducked inside the bag and sat down.

"Jerry, I'm going away for a few days, okay? Do you think you can handle the phones for me?"

Her brother nodded and gave her the thumbs-up. The phone rang and he answered, "Wright Enterprises. How can I help you?"

She smiled at him. "Good job. Don't let them take over, you hear me?"

He winked and went to work. Turning, she took two steps, and saw Hunter again, carrying her purse, clearly unhappy.

"Are you an accountant?" she asked him.

"Among other things. Today I'm here to escort you to—"

"Out of town," she said, glancing at Jerry.

"That's correct," he said, picking up her cue for

discretion. She wished he would step all the way back to the elevator so she could breathe, but to ask him would be rude. "Do you have a license?"

"For what?" he asked.

"Do you have one?"

"Yes."

"May I see it?"

He seemed to be considering her from behind reflective sunglasses. "If you don't mind, could you think a little faster?"

The only way she could tell she'd annoyed him was by the quirk in his jaw muscle.

Finally he pulled out his wallet and handed her his license.

"Here," she said, giving him Willa's arm as she scooted behind the receptionist's desk and scanned his ID into the computer. Vincent Hunter Smith, six foot two, black eyes, black hair, thirty-three years-old.

He was handsome, but scary.

"Ma'am?" he said. "We need to get a move on now."

"Alexandria. That's my name. Or you can call me Mrs. Wright-Foster."

"We don't have much time, Alexandria. We need to go now."

Somehow she hadn't thought he'd go for Mrs. even though he was older than her by ten years. "I'm coming," she said.

She returned his ID and he returned Willa, who'd lowered her sadness to a moan.

They boarded the elevator, and Willa stood behind them. "I don't think I'm going to find another job. I'm going to lose my apartment."

"Shh," Alex told her. "Willa, you'll work for me now as my personal assistant. Now be quiet. We have to think."

"About what?" Willa asked.

Alex stood next to Hunter who watched the numbers above their heads intently.

"I don't know," she replied. "But I think we should be having important thoughts."

He stuck his finger in his ear and shook rapidly.

They exited and got into his waiting SUV.

Maybe he'd gone swimming yesterday and the water wasn't all out.

"You should try earplugs when you go swimming."

His mirrored glasses turned toward her. "Buckle up. Where do you live?" he asked.

"Decatur, near the square."

"I know where that is."

"Good. The sooner we find out this was a mistake, the sooner I can go back to being Mrs. Marc Foster."

He glanced at her. "What if that doesn't happen?"

"I don't know who I'll be without him."

Chapter 2

LAX teemed with people, but Hunter only had eyes for one person.

His gaze was fixed on Alexandria who walked in a purposeful circle, BlackBerry in hand. They'd arrived at the departure gate fifteen minutes earlier, but the plane to Del Rosa hadn't arrived yet.

He wanted to check in with Chris, but didn't want to be overheard by the surprisingly stoic young woman. He'd expected a lot of questions during the flight from Atlanta. But after they'd gotten settled in first class—she'd won that argument as soon as they'd arrived at the airport—she'd fallen asleep almost immediately, her eyes covered by a black silk mask, a custom-made contoured pillow protecting her neck, her personal blanket tucked around her shoulders.

To be honest he'd been disappointed. He'd expected questions, and he'd prepared answers. But that was the problem. He hadn't had the opportunity to console the woman he'd been able to ascertain from his hurried investigation was a bit on the flighty, spoiled, entitled side.

As soon as they'd boarded the flight to California, she'd gotten comfortable, not wanting to eat or even drink anything except mineral water. Then she'd reclined her seat, tucked her hand under her chin, her neck against her pillow, and had fallen asleep.

Her beauty was flawless like that of a black porcelain doll, natural big black curls cascading over her shoulder nearly to her breasts. His mind began to play tricks on him as the plane streaked through the sky.

In his mind he'd taken her to Spain and Egypt, Russia and Europe. At first thought it had been an act, her falling asleep so perfectly. But then ten minutes rolled into a half hour, and then an hour, and then he realized he was the only one in their section not watching the movie or asleep. He'd been staring at her off and on for two hours.

Hunter stretched his back, relieved. To be off the plane and out of Atlanta felt good, but now Alexandria was attracting attention.

"I'll make sure our connection is on time," he said to give himself the benefit of distance.

"Where exactly are you going?" she asked, her eyes rich and vibrant, like the flavor cinnamon.

He looked at the desk and attendant five feet away. "Right there."

Maybe she was confused, he thought, giving her the benefit of the doubt. She'd just found out her husband was dead.

"I'm going to try Marc's phone again."

"If you wait a couple minutes, I'll find a place where you can make your call in private."

"I don't want to wait. I want to talk to him now."

"I understand that, Alexandria. Just give me a minute—"

"Hunter, I'm not a child. You don't have to babysit me."

What would happen if this was the time that she finally realized he was dead and she fell apart? Then he'd have an hysterical woman on his hands. What if Chris had been wrong and Marc answered the phone? Then he'd have an hysterical woman on his hands.

What was he thinking?

Marc was dead!

Alexandria was sucking him into her land of make-believe where there were toy dogs, sobbing assistants and lunatic family members, not to mention the queen bee herself, Alexandria. The Clampets had nothing on the Wrights.

Hunter moved forward in the line. If he didn't stick to the facts, he'd be as batty as they were. Marc was dead, he was escorting her to California, and in a few days, he'd be going back to Atlanta to resume running his security firm and playing his saxophone.

He'd finally gotten an offer to play at a small restaurant. The idea of taking his hobby to the public was the coolest feeling. Like he was some hotshot sax player.

He'd been waiting for that day for a long time. The movement in his arm was nearly a hundred percent after being paralyzed three years ago. Now his life was his own and he was ready to live it on his own terms.

Hunter checked the perimeter, being patient.

He'd be back in Atlanta soon, and all this crazi-
ness would be behind him.

Chris had been right. Alexandria wasn't pretty.
She was gorgeous, and that was causing a problem.

Passengers who'd been relaxing with their legs
outstretched snatched them back as if she were
Moses and they were the Red Sea. She threaded
her way through them and stopped at the window.
Once more she banged the phone against her
palm, put it to her ear, then dialed again.

The irrational feeling of wanting to abandon
his place in line seized him and Hunter understood the instinctual emotion. He'd worked in
security for nearly ten years. He'd protected
families of presidents, dignitaries and kings, and
now that he was in the private sector, sitting in his
office issuing instructions got boring. He was
being overprotective.

"How soon will the flight to Del Rosa be
boarding?"

"The plane just arrived," the attendant
Brittney answered with a smile that hinted at
recent injections. "We should be boarding in
about fifteen minutes."

Brittney was a cute blonde, but not his type. He
needed a woman on the East Coast, older than

him, and someone with career demands so high she didn't really need him.

"Your ticket, please?" Brittney offered him a look that held untold promises. He handed her both itineraries.

"Your wife?" she asked, her head tilted sideways. Jealousy lurked in her blue eyes, and he could see the explosive arguments before they happened. Accusations would fly like dessert plates, his CDs innocent victims of her rage.

Two men stood on either side of Alex, blocking her path. She tried to get around them, but they were playing a game of cat and mouse.

"Girlfriend?" Brittney sounded more hopeful, and he was rewarded with a fluttering of eye blinks.

"No, ma'am," he answered. "I'm her body-guard. Excuse me."

Hunter accepted the tickets, grabbed the jewel-toned designer purse that looked out of place on the vinyl seat, the empty doggie bag, neck pillow and magazines, and made his way over to the unlikely group. He stepped between the men and took her hand. "Mrs. Wright-Foster, we're ready to go."

"These men stopped me from getting by." She was breathless and looked close to tears.

"They're moving now." There was steel in his voice and Hunter knew he was invested in her. He'd hoped it was just in protecting her until he delivered her to the brother-in-law she'd never met, but he'd surpassed that level of impassioned professionalism four hours ago.

"I'm going to give you two scenarios," he said to the man wearing the terrible floral-shirt-patched-baggy-denim short combination. "One, you can spend the rest of your holiday as a guest of the Department of Homeland Security being questioned for unlawful imprisonment, or two, you can step aside and go on about your business."

Alexandria crowded him, her body seeking protection. There wouldn't be a fight, he knew, but these weren't the type of men to back down without a few words.

"She looked like she needed a real man to help her."

The words were meant to bait, but he wasn't biting.

"Don't worry, Officer," a young man of about twelve said, holding up his video camera. "I recorded everything."

"Thank you." Hunter never took his eyes off the man he sensed would be the most trouble.

Slowly they stepped back and once they sat down, the tension eased.

Just then Brittney announced that boarding would be delayed another fifteen minutes.

Hunter tipped his videographer, who happily showed the money to his mother, who waved her consent.

"That was really nice of you."

"He's a good kid. Hold on," he said, spotting a police officer. He pulled out his ID and the paperwork he'd received from Chris. "I'm looking for this lounge." They were directed out of the main area of the airport to a long hallway with doors on the right wall.

Alex hurried by his side, her skirt forcing her to take baby steps. "Hunter, I have something to say."

"You can't walk and talk at the same time?" Realizing he needed to be more sensitive, he stopped. "What is it?"

"Why are you so angry?"

"I'm not angry. Do you always attract that type of attention?"

"What? Those men? I can't help it if they wouldn't let me by."

"I told you to just give me a minute and I'd help you with your phone."

"I'm not a child. I don't need help." She sounded as irritated as he felt.

"Fine. Was that all you wanted to say?"

"No. You look funny carrying my purse on your shoulder."

Relief filled him and he realized he'd braced himself to be criticized by her. He thought she was going to complain that he'd embarrassed her or treated her badly. He'd heard it all before.

But not Alexandria. She was oblivious to her sex appeal. He handed her the pink purse. "You shouldn't leave your bag lying around."

"Thanks for rescuing me. I've been practicing how to become more assertive. But sometimes I get intimidated and the right words don't come out."

She had to practice being assertive? He'd never met a woman who didn't know how to assert her opinion about any and everything. And she'd handled her family pretty well considering they were all crazy.

"How were you going to be assertive against those men," he asked, looking at his watch, noting they only had about five minutes. Still, the quiet hallway was better than the main area of the airport.

"I would have said, 'If you don't get out of my way, I'm going to hurt you.'"

He tried to keep his smile hidden. "Hurt them…" He chuckled. "How?"

She put her hand on his shoulder and lifted her foot behind her. He endured her closeness and looked over her shoulder.

"This heel is a spike, and they had on those cheap flip-flops. One step in the right direction, and they'd have been on their knees."

"You're right about that," he said, liking the length of her hair, the feel of her hands on his shoulders and the closeness of her body to his. He cleared his throat. "It's time to board."

Turning, Alexandria started back up the hallway. Hunter trailed, watching her sexy heels. He stopped his gaze from continuing, because this relationship would end in less than a day.

Once settled on the flight, he pulled out his cell phone and listened to his messages.

There was no first-class on this flight, so they sat together, Alexandria continuously pressing buttons on her phone during the trip.

"Did you ever figure out the problem?" he asked.

"Someone had it cut off."

"What?" Hunter said.

"My phone's cut off. I'm trying to figure out how to pay it if it's cut off, but I don't know any bank account information. Marc paid our bills, I think, or maybe the accountant. May I use your phone? I need to call Mr. Feinstein."

Hunter handed it over, thinking high living at its worst. Alexandria fumbled through her Black-Berry, her hands shaking.

"Take a deep breath," he said, covering her hands with his. "Everything is going to work out."

"No it isn't, Hunter. My husband might be dead, I have a brother-in-law I don't know, and my phone is off. My world is coming to an end and everybody knows it but me. Do you not see how serious this is?"

The older couple in the seats ahead of them turned around and looked at Alexandria. "You're being rude," she snapped at them. "This is a personal conversation."

"You're the one who's talking loudly," the woman said with a scraggly voice and quickly turned around.

Hunter leaned close to Alex. "If you don't want people to hear what you're saying, just bring it down a little."

"We're practically in their laps. It's hard not to hear each other, but it's rude not to pretend."

He got real close again, breathing in an intoxicating blend of jasmine and lavender. "Look, everyone knows your business because you keep putting it out there."

"Your breath is tickling my ear."

He couldn't tell her what part of her was tickling his libido. "Just trying to share some wisdom," he said, eyeing the two-carat diamond and the pretty lobe it was attached to.

"Hello, it's Alexandria Lord Wright-Foster," she said, holding the pillow close to her mouth.

She pushed her shoulder forward, her head back and looked at him.

Hunter nodded, letting her know no one else could hear her but him.

"I have a problem," she told the person on the phone. "Service to my BlackBerry has been disconnected. Can you have it reactivated within a half hour? Thank you. Yes, I'll call you first thing tomorrow. We can discuss all the finances then. Thanks, goodbye."

"Problem solved," he asked, accepting his phone.

"Yes."

She still looked troubled, but pulled a little bottle from her bag and stopped the male flight attendant with a girlie flip of her fingernails. "May I have a bottle of water?"

"In just a few minutes. Ooh. Is that little ditty bag from Neiman's? The new misting and moisturizing solution?" he asked as she slid the tiny container from the velvet bag.

"Yes. You need a little freshening?"

The attendant's eyes lit up like Christmas had come again. "Always."

He hurried to the front and got an eight ounce bottle of water. On his return, he carefully poured about a dropper full into Alexandria's mister and she shook, then squeezed the atomizer at her face.

Hunter looked closely, but didn't see the difference.

"Hunter, do you want some?"

"No way."

Her purposeful blinks and pursed lips seemed to say that she was going to ignore him, and she passed it to the attendant. "You can have that as a present."

The attendant practically leaped for joy as he misted his face and neck. "Wow, thanks. You're so adorable." He touched Hunter's shoulder. "Don't you just want to eat her up?"

The image that comment evoked was too dangerous to consider. He cleared his throat. "How long is the flight?"

"Thirty minutes. I'd better get back to work. Thank you, doll," he said to Alexandria, and hurried about his duties.

Alexandria folded her hands, sat back and closed her eyes.

"What are you doing now?" he asked.

"Thinking important thoughts."

"Of course you are." He sat back and tried to do the same, like how soon was he going to get back to Atlanta and his real life?

Chapter 3

Hunter signaled the limousine driver who held a placard with their names on it. He'd retrieved their luggage, except for the dog.

"Alexandria, come with me." Hunter escorted her to the car and watched her slide against the seat, then swing her legs inside the limousine.

There was such class about her, but he wondered how much trouble she was capable of stirring up? He'd seen just a bit of it, but he wondered if this was the calm before or the eye of the storm.

He shut the door then went to the trunk with the driver. "What's your name?"

"Frazier." The driver shook his hand and they stored the bags in the trunk.

"I've got everything except the dog. Here's the slip."

"I'll get him now."

Hunter nodded, baffled as to why Chris had chosen a black stretch limousine for an airport run. It was overkill.

Climbing inside, he sat next to Alexandria who was in the middle of the backseat and hadn't moved an inch since she'd gotten in.

"I need to talk to Chris," Alexandria said.

Hunter realized he shouldn't have gotten in. The car was dark and private, and intimate.

"You will, very soon."

"Now, Hunter. I want to talk to him now." She didn't raise her voice as her father did, but her intention was no less direct.

"Chris is busy and can't talk to you until this afternoon. We only have time for you to get to the hotel, shower, change and ride to the chapel."

"He's not dead. For some reason, he canceled my phone."

Alexandria pulled out her phone and began to dial Marc's number again.

Hunter covered her hands with his, eased the

phone away and pocketed it. She looked down as if he'd just performed a magic trick. "Hunter?"

"I'm going to check on Little Sweetie for you, okay?"

"Okay." She reached for his pocket. "I want my phone back. Now that it's working, I need to make some calls."

"No more calls for now."

"No, I need my phone."

"Alexandria, we've traveled all this way. Have I hurt you? Have I done anything that wasn't in your best interest?"

"No."

"I'm asking you to trust me now."

"But—" She looked out the window, her hands empty. "How am I supposed to be assertive and take charge of my life when no one will let me?" She pouted and he braced for a tantrum, but there was no storm. The fight left as it came. And he felt as if he was the bad guy. No better than her father or brother. But he knew the day was going to get worse before it got better. He knew but she wouldn't believe him if he told her.

"We have guardian angels that protect us and we don't know it."

She tucked her chin. "You don't believe in guardian angels."

"I wouldn't be here without them. I took a bullet once—"

Hunter stopped, having never told anyone besides the veterans' psychologists about how it felt to be shot and paralyzed. The fact that he could use his right arm at all was a miracle. "I'm normal because of good doctors and great angels."

"Where?"

"I was in Fallujah." He realized that the intimacy of the limousine may have contributed to the revelation of such a private confession, so he focused on the foot traffic outside the window.

"I mean where on your body?" She touched him. "Your shoulder. Leg? Where?"

"My shoulder and, um, arm."

"Didn't you have a vest?"

"Yeah I did, but it just slowed the bullet."

"Then you know how I feel. I want this to be different. I don't want to know anything bad is going to happen."

"I know, Alex. Alexandria."

"You can call me Alex or Lexi."

"Here comes Frazier, our driver." Hunter stepped

out of the car and closed the door, accepting Little Sweetie's carrying bag. "How far is the hotel?"

"Fifteen minutes. Another ten to Flowers Memorial Chapel."

"Good. Let's get there as quickly as possible."

Hunter pulled Little Sweetie's bag of treats from the trunk and took a deep breath. He lifted the case so he could see the dog. The poor thing looked terrified. *Who needed the psychologist now?*

"You need to distract her for fifteen minutes. Do you think you can do that?" Hunter felt silly talking to the canine.

The animal yipped. "You need to learn how to bark like a real dog." He yipped again. "You're gay, aren't you?" Little Sweetie yipped again and wagged his tail.

Hunter smiled. "All right, little guy. Just distract her."

Frazier grinned at him. "You're funny, sir. Are you ready?"

"Let's roll. Fast."

The man winked. "Got you."

Hunter got inside and Alexandria's eyes brightened. "Little Sweetie!"

She reached for the case and the dog yipped all the way to her lap.

Hunter sat back, relieved.

He didn't dare pull out his phone and check the reason it was vibrating like crazy. But he didn't like the feeling in his feet that said run. Like he'd gotten in Fallujah.

They drove down a side street, stopping at the light, and a woman with a shopping cart walked up and peered into the back window of the car. She looked as if she'd been outside for years, her face and hands as worn and dirty as her wool coat.

Little Sweetie went crazy and Hunter reached out and covered his mouth. "Hush."

The dog kept it up.

"Shh," Alexandria said and he stopped. "What's she doing?" She turned into him, as if the woman was going to get in.

"Nothing." He put his hand on her leg and felt a whole lot of strong quadriceps. "She's just trying to see who's inside. She's not going to hurt you."

Little Sweetie yipped and Alexandria hushed him again. He went back into his bag and lay down.

The lady rifled through her cart and came out with a cardboard sign that she clothespinned to the side of her cart.

Beware of the man with the hole in his heart.

The driver turned the corner, drove another mile and stopped at the exclusive Black Diamond Hotel.

"Did that just freak you out or what?" Alexandria wondered aloud, shaking her shoulders.

"No, not at all."

"I always pay attention to signs and the metaphysical. You know, things out of this world." Her smile was sad. "Don't you?"

"From her? I don't know that she'd be a reliable source." Hunter shook his head. "I rely on reality."

"Yeah, but sometimes messages come from strange places," she said, and was about to say more.

Their door was opened by a valet in a black coat, and Alexandria and the dog alighted. Their bags were removed from the trunk and taken inside.

Check-in had been taken care of electronically by the driver who'd alerted the hotel upon their arrival at the airport.

Hunter was impressed. All they had to do was sign, and they were escorted to a bank of elevators, then to the seventh floor.

"I'll come for you in thirty minutes. Is that enough time?" Hunter asked.

"Forty is better," she said. "I want to give Little Sweetie time to stretch his legs."

Hunter nodded. "Forty then. The weather's supposed to be cool. You might want to wear a coat."

"Thank you. I'll be ready."

He waited for the valet to step out of the room, then tipped the man. "Alexandria? Don't keep me waiting."

"I wouldn't do that. Where's your room?"

He looked at the card and pointed. "Right next door. I've got it from here," he said to the valet, shouldering his duffel bag.

Hunter let himself in, followed by Alexandria.

"Do we have adjoining rooms?"

"I don't think so," he said, but then he saw the door. He'd hoped not. Not that they'd use it. But the door implied intimacy the same way the dark windows in the limousine had. "I stand corrected."

"Good. So if I need you, I can just open this door." Alexandria unlocked it and turned around, Little Sweetie following her. "Don't keep *me* waiting, Hunter."

He watched her go. "I won't."

Behind his closed door, he unpacked and showered within fifteen minutes then dialed Chris, but got his voice mail.

Hunter rubbed his hair, thinking of the bag

lady's sign. Nobody knew how superstitious he was. He held his hand over his heart as he'd done a thousand times since last month. His heart was beating fine.

The lady's sign had freaked him out.

Until two months ago, he'd had arterial septal defect, better known as a hole in his heart.

Surgery had fixed the defect, but if Alexandria knew, she'd probably have gotten out of the limo and walked back to the airport. They wouldn't be at the hotel on the way to the funeral of the husband she refused to believe was dead, and she wouldn't have an adjoining room.

The door on the other side unlocked but didn't open.

He took his medicine and stored the pills in his suitcase that he'd have to take for the rest of his life. This was something Alex would never know about.

He didn't need her to regress to the suspicious looks, and the cold way she'd been, having Willa watch him with the phone in her hand, 911 dialed, her finger poised over the Send button if he made a wrong move while in her condo yesterday.

They'd built up a level of trust. He just needed that to continue until tomorrow.

Then he'd return to Atlanta and she'd go back to her crazy family.

Dressing, Hunter put on his suit and was ready in twenty minutes. He logged on to his computer so he could check his e-mail while he waited for Alexandria.

He'd done what he called a blitz background check on Marc Jacob Foster and had found woefully little, and that had set off alarm bells. It was as if the man hadn't existed before two years ago.

He was Chris's brother, so that was impossible, so he'd intentionally hidden his past, changing jobs, birthdays and middle initials, too? He was definitely hiding something.

Marc owned several homes. Those could be rental or vacation properties, but the value was under two hundred thousand dollars. Certainly not something Alexandria would call luxurious.

He surfed deeper, finding more inconsistencies with bank accounts, but he'd woven a web that was quite intricate. Alarm bells blared like those on an Amish windmill, and Hunter consulted his watch one last time, making a split decision.

This wasn't his case. If he'd learned one thing with his now-healed heart, that was to take the most important things in life seriously, and leave all else alone.

He changed his flight to leave tomorrow.

He printed his boarding pass and left it on the table.

Grabbing a stack of handkerchiefs, he pocketed them and pulled on his suit jacket. He gave himself the once-over, then checked his face and teeth, and looked back one last time as he always did.

The boarding pass was where he'd left it. Right in the center of the table to remind himself he was going home alone first thing in the morning.

Chapter 4

Flowers Memorial Chapel was a quaint white and blue building. Planters of neatly manicured evergreen bushes lined a discreet path to the back of the building as the driver parked in front between even white lines. A ray of sunlight kissed blooming pink and fire-red cymbidium, distracting Hunter from the somber reason for their visit. Silence hugged them and he waited, knowing what Alex was feeling. He'd lost both his mother and father too young, and he remembered sitting in a freezing Chevy Caprice, looking at the wilted flowers in his sister's hand, waiting for her to tell him it was all a mistake. Her eyes hadn't lied when she'd looked at him.

"We're here?" Alexandria asked him as she absently pet her dog.

"Yes. Do you want to sit here for a few more minutes?" The heater was on, the engine still running. Although it was California, the weather was colder than Atlanta by at least fifteen degrees.

Alex shrugged her shoulders as if the move was costing her physically. "No. Let's go inside."

Hunter tapped once on the window and Frazier opened the door.

"Hunter?" She still hadn't moved and he wondered why no one had called her to see if she were all right. Where were her friends? Her mother? Why was she here all alone with him?

"Yes?"

"My phone, please."

The last thing he wanted was to fight with her. But why would she need it? "We're about to go inside. Why don't we go back to the hotel, and you can talk to anyone you'd like then."

"Now, please?"

"Really, Alex, you don't need it."

She shook her hand at him and said nothing.

"You're like Dr. King. A peaceful resister."

"If you say so."

"Don't use it in there."

"Don't tell me what to do, Hunter."

Had she fought like a hellcat, he'd have an argument and when he'd run out of arguments, he'd have simply ignored her, but her cool-under-pressure approach got to him.

Now he felt out of control.

Hunter finally handed the phone to her. Stepping from the car, he offered her a hand out.

She alighted with her hat securely in place and tipped her head back to see him.

"You sure you don't want to leave that thing in the car," he asked, the wide brim making a dramatic statement.

"That's a silly question. It matches my dress."

He hadn't seen the dress, her coat so long it was nearly to her ankles. They walked up the steps and he opened the door, allowing her to walk in sideways. Every move she made was delicate and smooth. But she seemed apprehensive. "Which way do I go?"

An attendant approached. "Your name, please?"

"Mrs. Marc Foster. This is Mr. Hunter Smith."

The man opened his mouth like a gaping fish,

then he closed it. Holding out his hand, he guided them to a room at the far end of the chapel. "Please proceed inside when you're ready. Ma'am, may I take your coat?"

"Of course." Alex unbuttoned the silk, transferring her purse from one hand to the other while Hunter helped her slide her arms from the sleeves. She stepped forward and he swallowed his surprise.

The sleeveless dress was white with black polka dots. A white silk sash bustled slightly from the waist to her knees. The dress probably cost more than a suite at the Four Seasons, but that wasn't what he was concerned about. It wasn't exactly appropriate for a funeral.

The attendant, again, didn't say a word. He gestured to show Hunter where the coat would be stored and hurried off.

"White, Alexandria," he said. "This *is* a funeral."

"I don't believe it's my husband. So why should I wear black?"

She took her bag from him, and on impossibly high heels, walked up the center aisle.

Following at a discreet distance, Hunter slid onto a chair and sat down. Alex was no longer his responsibility. If she'd worn an ice blue-colored dress with orange shoes, a pink hat and purple dots on her skin, that wouldn't be his problem.

Except she'd look like a clown at a rodeo. And he knew what a nice clown she could be. She'd been nice to Willa and to him, and even to Jerry, her brother, so he felt sorry for her as she stood at the first row of chairs still and quiet.

He got up and walked toward her as the only attendant in the room approached. "Would you like to sit for a moment, ma'am?"

Her fingers stroked the air as if she was playing the keys on a piano, and he backed away.

She eased closer and Hunter moved too, knowing he meant nothing to her, but how could he call himself a man and not be there for her when she had no one else?

Softly whispered words reached his ears and he listened to the pleas for this man to not be her husband. He listened until her begging stopped.

"I'm right here," he said.

"I'm a big girl. Let me be."

Hunter took a seat on the front left row, unoccupied but close enough he could reach her if she broke down. But as she stood there, he wondered when that would be. She hadn't cried once.

"Marc, you really are dead. What am I going

to do now? Who's going to help me now? You told me you didn't have a brother or any family at all. Why did you lie to me?"

Plaintive and calm, her voice carried, even though she wasn't speaking loud. She sounded as if Marc was standing right there, but that was the problem, he wasn't. Hunter suspected she was about to crack.

"You're just like my father and brother, and you said you weren't like them. I wish I could make you look at me and tell me why—" Her voice broke then. "What else have you lied about?"

Another couple sat in the section across from Hunter and the man nodded a greeting, while the woman stared at Alex's back, her face pained.

"I could never love a liar. Maybe that's what happened," Alex said, and Hunter rose. She took a step back right into his chest.

Little Sweetie barked, startled by the jarring motion.

"What in the world is that?" the woman from the front row demanded.

"My dog," Alex mumbled, still looking at Marc's dead face. "He gave me Little Sweetie so I wouldn't be lonely. Marc traveled so much with his job."

The man had stood to steady Alex. She was clearly upset, but still hadn't shed a tear.

"I've got her," Hunter said, hoping to guide her out of the chapel and back to the car. "Hunter Smith," he said softly, extending his hand, leaning away from Alex's hat.

"Tristan Adams. Good to meet you."

"You, too."

Alex turned from looking at Marc, the discussize hat in everybody's way. "I'm Alexandria Lord Wright-Foster. Marc's wife. And you are Marc's sister," she asked, holding out her hand. "I didn't know he had a brother, so I'm so surprised to meet you too."

"I'm *Mrs.* Danielle Timmons-Foster," the woman said, rising from the chair. "Marc's wife."

Alexandria looked up. Danielle was a tall, striking woman who reminded Hunter of Angela Bassett. He'd seen this woman in magazines for years. She'd been a model, but she'd disappeared a year ago.

Today grief and now anger creased her exotic eyes, and she didn't look as if she would hold her tongue. He just didn't think she knew she'd met her match in Alex.

Hunter reached for Alex, who looked at his hand

and patted it as if he needed comfort. He shook his head. "Your hat," he said, rearing back as it caught him on the chin. "It's hitting everyone."

She swiveled and he leaned back again.

"Oh, is it?"

Alex turned around and everyone gave her a two foot berth.

She removed it and her hair cascaded down in full natural curls.

Danielle rolled her eyes.

"Do you mean you *were* Marc's first wife?" Alexandria asked.

"No, I mean I'm still married to him," Danielle said, and pressed into the tiny circle. She was eased back by Tristan, who seemed patient and caring.

"There must be some mistake, because *I'm* married to him," Alex said confidently.

"That's impossible," another woman said who walked up, her voice softer than the others. "I'm Renee Mitchell-Foster, Marc's *current* wife."

Renee was tall too, but she was different than the other two. Where Danielle was a sexy model, and Alex a young beauty, Renee was ultraconservative. A severe black boxy skirt stopped at her knees, while an equally square jacket hung off her shoulders. He didn't know Mary Jane

T-strap shoes were still being made, but she'd found a pair, and a double strand of white pearls draped her throat. She gripped a sensible black purse right at her breast and fisted her other hand at her side.

"Librarian?" Alex asked.

"How did you know?" Renee replied.

"Your suit says you got it at the mall, but your shoes were a dead giveaway." Alex sounded Southern and uppity. "That dead man is my husband and we got married last year. Our anniversary was just last month. I know this is a sad day for everyone, but as his last official wife, I'd like a few minutes alone with my husband."

"You're not the spokesperson for *my husband*. I've been married to him for five years," Danielle said. "And I have the marriage certificate to prove it. We never got divorced." Danielle produced the paper and they each leaned in to look at it.

The music paused then started again. A door in the back closed and the air stirred, but the room had a tomblike feeling, as if they were the only people in the entire building.

Hunter couldn't wait to get out of there.

"I'm Marc's wife of two years." Renee lifted her

chin as if she could take a knock or two from a heavyweight champion. "This is the picture of our wedding and honeymoon in Opelika, Alabama."

"Not that Mecca," Danielle said, clearly unimpressed.

"We're not all rich like you, and I might buy my clothes at the mall, but I won't be intimidated just because you have more expensive garments or live in fancy places, *Mrs.* Timmons-Foster. So if you want to have a problem with me, go higher on the food chain of insults, got it?"

"Wow, that was good," Alex said, smiling at Renee. "I wish I could say things like that." Both women looked at Alexandria. "What did I do?" She put her hands on her hips. "I didn't bring any certificates or pictures. All I've got is me. Should I get naked and show you every place Marc celebrated on our wedding and anniversary?"

The other two turned their heads. "Good grief no," Renee said, turning her back.

"All righty then. I was married to him a year ago. I don't know what happened, but he must have divorced you two and you didn't know it. He's my husband, and I want you two gone," Alex said.

Little Sweetie started to yip. "Shh," Alex told him, jiggling her bag.

"Why do you have a dog here?" Danielle snapped.

"Marc bought him for me as a gift, and now he's my Little Sweetie. So that's what I named him. He's like my child and my best friend all rolled into one. You brought yours and I don't have a problem with that, so why do you have a problem with mine?" Little Sweetie yipped away. Alexandria sounded as if she wanted to cry. "He's getting upset because you're both stressing me out." She shushed him and jiggled his bag until he quieted. Then she reached inside the pocket and gave him a treat.

Another door closed and Chris hurried up the aisle.

"Chris," Hunter said. "It's about time. We've been waiting."

"I'm sorry you had to meet this way. I'm Chris Foster. Marc's brother."

"Marc told me he didn't have any family," they all said, practically in unison.

The silence was uncomfortable and long. Without planning to, all three ladies stood side by side looking at Chris, then at Marc in his casket.

"You resemble him," Danielle said. "But that's it."

"You're younger," Alex said. "Less stressed. You work out, I can tell."

Chris nodded.

"Oh, my God," Danielle said. "Is she hitting on him?"

"Who me?" Alex asked.

"You don't look anything like Marc," Renee said emphatically, caught up in the moment. "I don't see that at all. I can tell you're possibly related, but that's it. Were there any personal effects?"

"Pardon?" Chris asked, looking at Hunter. He shrugged.

"Was there anything found with the body?" Renee asked again.

"Yes. His briefcase and a few other items in his plane. But nothing substantial. We can talk about that later."

"I don't want to be here later. I want to get everything over with now." Renee was firm and concise.

She wasted a movement smoothing hair that was in a tight bun as she kept her gaze locked on Marc's face.

Chris went and stood by Renee's side. "There's too much to talk about now. I'm sorry to have to do this, but I need everyone to stay at least a day so we can talk this out. Can everyone meet tonight at five at the hotel?" he suggested.

"Can we say six? It's been a long flight from Florida. We're a little jet-lagged." Tristan spoke for both himself and Danielle. His arm slid over her shoulder in a gentle hug. "Let's sit over here a few minutes. Then we'll step out and let the other ladies have their time."

Danielle's eyes were red, but they narrowed to slits when she looked at Alex. "Fine, but she and the dog have to go." Danielle barely glanced at Renee. "I don't care what you do."

Renee gasped.

"Danielle…" Tristan's rebuff was strong enough to stop her forward motion.

"I don't care, Tristan."

"Yes, you do."

Hunter wondered what else was going on between the couple. At first he'd thought they were brother and sister, but they were shoulder to shoulder, and Tristan looked down at her as if he knew her better than he knew himself. Only she didn't realize it.

"Ms. Thing had one thing right," Danielle said. "He's a dead liar."

"But it's not their fault, and it's not yours."

"You don't know, Tristan." Danielle stared at Marc's peaceful body. He had no idea the hornet's nest he'd left behind. Or maybe he did. "They could be in on this," Danielle said.

"What? Being shocked and surprised that he's dead? I don't think so. Do you want me to stay or do you want a few minutes alone?" Tristan asked her.

Hunter was at the back of the chapel by then. He decided right then that he liked Tristan. He didn't take any mess and he didn't engage in arguments he couldn't settle right away.

Chris and Renee lagged behind them about ten feet. "Alexandria? Is six okay?"

"Fine," she said without turning around.

"Come on, sweetheart." The words were out of Hunter's mouth before he could stop them. He guided Alex from the room. She passed under his nose, looking up at him with inquisitive eyes. "I'm sorry, he said. "I don't know where that came from."

"That's okay." Alex fingered her hat, looking in her bag at Little Sweetie. "Today's the second worst day of my life. So it seems right that the sweetest thing somebody has to say to me is on the wrong day. My coat, please."

Hunter didn't realize she'd walked him directly over to the coat room. "What are you doing?"

She put her bag on the floor between her feet, and Little Sweetie started jumping, playing with the bottom of her dress.

"I'm leaving." She pushed her arms through the sleeves and turned her back so he could help her get the coat over the back of her dress. She buttoned the coat down the front and belted it. The toile lay flat, just as it had on the way over. That's how he'd never seen it. Some investigator he was.

He was leaving, he reminded himself. This woman had distracted the hell out of him for the last time.

"Alex, we're not leaving." Hunter didn't want to examine the words that just contradicted the thought he had a moment ago. He didn't want to think about his printed boarding pass on the table back at the hotel. All he could think about was Alexandria Lord Wright-Foster not being pushed around again in two days.

"Yes, we are."

"Would you let another woman steal your man?"

"No," she said, walking toward the door, her doggie bag on her arm, her hat in her hand. "Not if I wanted him."

"He was your husband."

"I know."

"Did you want him?"

"I used to."

"Then fight to find out why he did what he did."

"Open the door for me. I'm going outside."

Hunter was about to say no. Generally, he stayed away from bossy women, but then he saw the pain etched in her face.

She swallowed.

Her lips pursed.

And the first tear fell. She whisked it away as if it was never there.

He opened the door.

"Don't follow me," she told him, and her hand landed softly in the center of his chest. Then, "Please, don't leave me."

"Okay."

Chapter 5

Alex rounded the hotel's track for the seventeenth time wishing she felt as good as she had on the thirteenth lap.

Who said thirteen was an unlucky number?

She pushed herself trying to obliterate the sound of Danielle's and Renee's voices from her mind. *Who were these people? Marc was a bigamist? That just didn't sound right. Poly– something or other?*

There was another name for a man who married more than two women, but she couldn't think of it.

Maybe she was dumb. Maybe her father was right. How could she not know her husband was married to two other women?

Wouldn't he have come home stinking of another woman? He would have avoided her gaze, told elaborate lies and had friends who covered for him. But Marc didn't have friends. He didn't have receipts or loose papers, and he didn't get any personal calls or business calls.

Marc didn't come home.

Alex stumbled, and her hands flew out to break her fall. Crashing to the ground, she screamed in pain, her left hand and knee taking the brunt of the fall. Before the full impact could radiate through her body, she was on her back and was looking at the gym's ceiling.

"Are you trying to kill yourself?" Hunter was over her, looking down, his voice calm yet concerned. His hands were on her shoulder and hip and he seemed almost on top of her. "What happened?"

"I was thinking and running fast, and I guess I was so deep in thought I tripped and fell. I'm sorry."

He chuckled. "You're apologizing to me? That's real nice of you, but that's not how it works. I get to say I'm sorry. Does anything hurt?"

She tried to raise her arm and winced. "My

hand and knee hurt." Alex tried to draw her knee up but froze with her leg half raised.

"Where exactly does it hurt?" Hunter supported her ankle with gentle fingers.

"Take off my kneecap and rub right there."

"You are so Southern," he said imitating her.

"I know. I used to get teased about my accent, but I guess I'm used to it."

A quick smile creased his lips and she decided to focus on his mouth to keep from crying. "You have nice teeth. Not all rotten and crooked like nobody cared about you. What do you think I should do?"

His eyebrows drew together for a second. "About my teeth or your leg?"

"My leg." She felt a smile start and wondered, after her day how smiling was even possible.

"If you'll let me touch everything but your kneecap, I'll be able to tell if anything leading to the kneecap is injured and maybe how bad. Then we'll decide if you can put any pressure on it. If you can walk out of here, we'll ice it. If you can't, then it's a trip to the E.R."

"How do you know all of this?"

"My first year in the army, I was a medic. Then when I got shot, I spent a lot of time in the veterans' hospital. So I've got lots of on-the-job training."

He pressed her quadriceps starting at her hip. "Here?" he asked, moving down the muscle in inch degrees. "Here?" he asked as he moved closer to her knee.

"There," she said loudly, "there, stop!"

She'd bolted upright and gripped his hand to her chest. She counted slowly waiting for her heartbeat to slow. Her knee hurt, but she knew she had to relax each muscle, and she started with her jaw and worked her way down.

Her lying, cheating jerk of a husband had just been buried, she assumed, she hadn't even stayed to see him in the ground, and she was letting another man touch her. What was happening to her life?

"I think you should see a doctor," he said gently, loosening her viselike grip on his hand. "I can carry you downstairs to a cab and take you to the hospital myself."

"No, no," she said, hearing her accent. "A hospital is out of the question."

Why didn't his suggestion surprise her? Everything she wanted to do, he thought the opposite. If she wasn't going home, she definitely wasn't going to a hospital.

"I'm not missing tonight's meeting." She tried to put pressure on her left hand, and aching pain caused her to wince and her eyes to tear. She closed her eyes, waiting for the silver stars to disappear. "No way."

"They'd understand that you're hurt."

"If I were them I wouldn't. They already think I'm stupid, and that Danielle hates me. Renee, I don't know about her yet."

Hunter tapped her hard on the shoulder until she jerked her shoulder away. "Ow! What!"

"Are you stupid?"

"No!"

"Are you dumb?"

"No."

"You're a lot of things, but stupid and dumb aren't any of them. Don't say it again."

The harshness of his reprimand hurt nearly as much as falling. "Don't tell me what to do."

"I'll tell you what to do or I'm going home tonight at nine."

"You'd leave me?"

Hunter looked down at her from his crouched position. Strands of hair had escaped her braid and he pushed them from her face. He seemed to be thinking so many things.

"If you're going to be self-destructive, I'm not going to watch."

"What if I can't do what you want?"

"You want to be treated well. Start by treating yourself well."

"Okay. Hunter, I want you to stay with me the next few days. I know that's a lot to ask, but I can pay you."

"I'm expensive, and I have a lot to do at home."

"Work? Can you get someone to stand in for you? Please. I don't have anyone. Please?"

"Three days is all I can do."

"Thank you." Impulse told her to hug him, but common sense told her to keep her hands to herself.

"But," he added, "if we aren't getting along, then we'll both know it's time for me to go. Come on. Let's take a look at your hand."

Alex extended it, and for the first time Hunter looked at her wedding set. He studied the rings for a few seconds and then he looked away.

Alex looked at her rings, too.

Two carats of diamonds surrounded a beautiful two-carat round solitaire that she'd been so proud of, until now. Suddenly a sickening heat slithered up her body, making her feel nauseous. "The diamonds aren't real."

Hunter didn't reply. He gingerly slid his fingers along hers and moved them in tiny degrees. "Any pain?" he asked.

"Hunter?"

"Can you bend your finger?" he said.

She didn't even try.

"Squeeze my fingers, Alex." He waited for her, and when she didn't, he looked frustrated. But no more than she felt. "Why aren't you cooperating?"

"Cooperation works both ways, Hunter."

He looked back at her hand. "No, they're not real."

"Do you have a side job as a jeweler?" Anger burst from her like an unexpected summer storm. "What don't you do? You're an accountant, medic, FBI agent, soldier, security person. Are you married? I mean, goodness, you'd be worth more than platinum to someone."

He didn't even seem flustered at her meltdown. "You pressed, remember? You had to know. Why are you shooting the messenger?"

"Don't you lie? Because, I'm going to tell you something, this would have been the time."

"No, I don't lie. Not as a general rule. Do you lie?"

"Of course I do. If you were me and had my day, I would have lied to spare me this scene right now. I would have said the diamonds are gorgeous. Have them appraised for your insurance, and then let the poor appraiser deliver the bad news."

"I don't live in that world."

"What world, Hunter? I tell the truth when it's important. But my husband just died. The lying, cheating, can't-get-enough-of-other-women husband who I thought only loved me. So I would have lied and told me my rings were real."

"You see, that's why I'm not married."

"Why not?" Some of her anger evaporated and she had no idea why.

"First because women are difficult creatures to understand, and second because I was taught honesty is the best policy. I'm sorry your rings aren't real, but he did it, not me. I worked for a jeweler when I was in high school and that's how I could tell the stones are cubic zirconia."

"What haven't you done?"

"One or two jobs. Those are classified."

Alex looked up at him, curled her hand around his and squeezed.

"Good. I don't think they're broken, but I still think you should be checked out by a doctor."

She tried to flex her hand. "Is everything about my life with Marc going to be a lie?"

"Do you want me to be honest?"

Alex could feel the muscles in her back and legs tensing, her stomach, and even her chest. She was afraid to say yes. But being so close to Hunter made her feel a little safer, at least temporarily. "Yes."

"You should probably prepare for that possibility."

She nodded. "Help me up, please. I choose not to believe that, you know. I believe there's an explanation for all of this."

"On three, I'm going to pull you up. One, two, three."

Alex was up and unsteady, her hands on his shoulders, Hunter's hands on her waist.

What she wanted at that very second was a good, long hug. But how could she ask for that? Her husband was dead. Her family was angry with her and she wanted to be comforted by Hunter. He'd just told her the truth and she'd gotten angry.

He'd told her the truth again and she'd denied wanting to know. When was real going to be real again? How would she ever be able to trust a man again?

"You don't believe in hoping for a better outcome, Hunter?"

"Yes. I wish this whole day had started and ended differently. Then you'd have an entirely different perspective.

"Step lightly and test the strength of your knee. I'll support your weight with my body. Lean on me. Now step."

Alex did as he instructed and her knee was weak, but it wasn't too bad.

She needed to be alone. So if the tears fell, she would be the only one that would know. "It feels okay. I can't run, but I think I'll be all right."

"I'll help you back to your room."

"If I hold on to the wall, I can make it back okay."

"But if you hold on to me, you'll make it back for sure."

She knew that. She needed some time away from Hunter. This whole day was too much for her and it wasn't even over.

"I don't want to stop you from working out."

"I'll get it in later," he said, yanking on her braid. "Come on. Last one back gets the ice."

Chapter 6

The conference room wasn't as nice as the one at Wright Enterprises, but Alex tried to get comfortable, her leg propped up on the chair next to her, Little Sweetie sleeping on her lap.

Money had been wasted on dinner nobody ate, as they sat at the conference table with Chris, shrouded in a veil of grief, confusion and suspicion.

Alex looked over at Hunter who stood at the window next to Tristan, and offered her a nod of moral support. He'd agreed to stay and that's all that mattered. This day felt as if it couldn't get any worse.

Chris shuffled the papers in front of him again. "Marc was my older brother by two years. We were born and raised in Costa Woods, California. We weren't close the past few years, but I wrote out a chronology that might fill in some of the inconsistencies."

"There aren't any inconsistencies," Alex interrupted. "He lied to us."

"How do we know you're not lying to us now?" Renee asked. "How do I know this isn't some elaborate scam?"

Chris rubbed his eyes and folded his hands in front of him on the table. "Yes, Marc lied. I don't know why. I'm the executor of a house of lies. I'm the younger brother to a liar, but that only makes my job superhard. As for scams, I'm not asking you for anything. He didn't have much life insurance to speak of. I found one policy and it's for ten thousand dollars. That's what I used to bury him. The rest came from my own pocket."

Chris opened a folder on the table and distributed copies to everyone. "Our mother took out this life insurance policy when we were children. Our mother, Betty Foster, is deceased now ten years. Our father, Spencer, is deceased, eleven years."

"There's a problem, Chris. I have a life insurance policy on Marc," Danielle said, "and I'll need a copy of the death certificate so I can collect the insurance money."

"So do I," Renee said forcefully. "But it has to be proven whose husband he is first."

"He's my husband. I'm sure of that. I have to check with my accountant, but I know we have life insurance, too," Alex told them.

"You should have married your accountant," Danielle said sarcastically.

"I thought about this today while I was getting a facial, Danielle. You're very pretty. But why would Marc marry a woman like you and then fool around on her? He asked to marry me last. Obviously he wasn't happy with you, and I can see why. You're a very unhappy person."

"You were getting a facial while we were *burying* your husband?"

"Yes, it calms me. Besides, Marc managed to do a lot of things without me, including have other wives and die," Alex said angrily.

"But if you loved him oh, so much, you'd have seen him to his final resting place."

"I didn't need to do that, Danielle. You were there. Did he get buried?" Alex stopped herself. Little Sweetie had an expression of alarm on his face. Alex realized that she was shouting. She sat back in her chair.

"Let's stick to business," Renee said into the stiff silence. "Legally, the real Mrs. Foster would be entitled to any and all insurance monies resulting from his death."

"Are you an attorney?" Danielle stared Renee down.

"No, but I do know a little about insurance policies."

"Nobody is getting any money that I paid for my husband's insurance policy." Danielle looked as threatened as she sounded.

Alex hated when Danielle looked at her for an extended period of time. She felt as if she was back in middle school and the teacher was asking a world-history question.

"If Marc's declared my legal husband, I'm entitled to the money. You ladies should know that I've already called my attorney, and as we speak, your assets are being frozen until this matter is settled," Renee announced, picking up her purse and standing.

Alex sat up and looked at her. "What did you say?"

"As of an hour ago I asked my attorney to have

your assets frozen until we sort out who is legally married to Marc and what assets are and aren't his."

Alex shook her head. "Renee, I wish you'd talked to me before doing that. Attorneys have their place, but they can sure complicate things. Just a minute. Let me take care of this." She pulled out her BlackBerry and pushed several buttons.

"Who are you calling in the middle of this meeting?" Danielle demanded.

"I'm not going to shout at you again, Danielle, but just hold on. I'm going to do you a favor, and one day you're going to thank me." Alex held up one finger. "Hey, Nelda, this is Alexandria Lord Wright-Foster calling for my godfather," she winked at Danielle, who rolled her eyes. Alex squinted and then focused on her manicure.

"Can he make himself available to me, please, for five minutes?" Alex laughed. "I know it's been a month of Sundays since I called. I will get by for dinner. Yes, I'll hold."

She put her hand over the mouthpiece. "I'll be just a minute more. It'll help you too, Renee… Godfather, it's me, Lexi. I'm having a bit of trouble and I need your help. My husband, Marc, died in a plane crash. Thank you, that's very kind. No, Daddy doesn't know yet. Here's the problem.

Marc was a total jerk and was married to two other women at the same time as he was married to me, and one of them has just informed me that's she's frozen my assets. I know, Godfather, it's all a horrible mistake. Can you please explain why that won't happen? I'm in a meeting right now with the other Mrs. Fosters. May I put you on speakerphone?"

Alex pushed the button and set it on the table. "Go ahead, Godfather."

"This is appellate court Justice Theodore Fitzhulme Thomas."

Shock registered on the faces of everyone in the room. All eyes moved between Alex and the phone on the table.

Alex wasn't sure what to make of Hunter's expression. He'd been surprised like everyone else, but now he seemed to have made a judgment and slipped behind his wall of indifference.

"Who am I speaking to?" Justice Thomas asked.

Each person stated their name and relationship to Marc.

"My condolences to all of you, because one way or another, your lives were affected somehow by Mr. Foster. Let me tell you something about my goddaughter. Lexi has more money than the president of a small bank. If you think you're going to stop her by attempting to freeze her assets, you'll need the services of an extremely large law firm, and a lot of financial resources. You should also know that you will lose because she has some of the best legal minds in the South at her disposal.

"Now, whatever your problems, work them out rather than financing your attorneys' next vacation home. Lexi's a better friend than enemy. As am I. Do you understand?"

A chorus of "yes, sirs" filled the room.

"I never met Marc, but he sounds like something I'd want off the bottom of my shoe. Ladies, consider yourselves lucky that you found out. Who knows," the judge went on, "there could have been more of you. Is there any other way I can help you?"

"How can we find out who Marc was legally married to?" Renee asked.

"I'd have all of your marital documents reviewed by a third-party law firm. They'll be able to analyze them and cut through the red tape, especially if any of you were married overseas or in the Caribbean. Anything else?"

"No sirs", abounded.

Alex picked up the phone. "Godfather, I'll call

you when I get back to Atlanta. Please don't tell Daddy that I called and why. He called you? I appreciate your support. Thank you so much. I love you too, bye now."

Alex set her phone down and rubbed Little Sweetie's back.

Danielle was glaring at her again.

"What did I do now, Danielle?"

"You don't have anything to say?"

"Chris, I apologize for interrupting your meeting. I wasn't trying to be unfriendly, Renee, but I don't like being threatened."

"Neither do I," she said, looking sad.

"I just want to know if Marc's my husband. I really need to know," Alex said, feeling insecure and shy.

"So do I," Renee said. "I apologize." She sounded as if she'd been defeated by Caesar. "I'll call my attorney as soon as I get to my room."

"You can use my phone," Alex offered. "I have free minutes."

Danielle groaned and pressed her fingers into the table. She didn't seem to have assertiveness problems. She had anger issues. But now wasn't the time to point that out. "Renee said she'll take care of it later. Can we move on?"

"Yes, let's," Chris said, although Alex sat forward, ready to defend herself. "Justice Thomas spelled it out for you. We need to have the documents verified. You're all on the East Coast, so I'd recommend a firm over there. However, the legal ramifications go deeper."

"Deeper?" Danielle asked. "How?"

"You've been filing taxes jointly and buying property. I've contacted Marc's employer and they do have a modest policy, but it seems my brother may have declined the larger life insurance portion he was entitled to take."

Renee covered her mouth, Danielle smacked the table and Alex shrugged.

"It defies reasoning," Danielle murmured, looking at Tristan, who'd remained quiet during the meeting.

"No, it demonstrates a level of selfishness I didn't know my husband possessed. I'm leaving tonight. I've heard enough."

Renee stood up and Tristan helped her as she bumped into the chair. "What else could there be?" She flapped her cotton shirt, her face growing damp. "This is ridiculous. What else could he possibly do to humiliate me more? Why would Marc do this? He stole from me. I'm a very logical person, but I don't understand why, how…" She touched her forehead. "I thought he loved me," she whispered.

"My wedding rings are cubic zirconia," Alex announced. "I found out today," she said more softly.

Each of the women looked at her own hand.

"You're kidding," Danielle said. "That was the only thing stopping me from hurling them into the ocean! I thought I could at least hock them. I hope his stinking soul is rotting in a landfill right now."

Renee laughed and looked at Danielle. "Really? A landfill? I thought you'd go straight for hell."

"I'm trying to stop cursing."

"You never curse," Tristan said, half smiling at her.

"I've been thinking about it. A lot." She turned her head defiantly.

Alex was amazed at her beauty. That "you can love me, but I'll leave you" look had made Danielle famous.

Renee slid her rings off her finger and stared at them. "How do you know yours are fake?" she asked Alex.

"I fell down in the gym and hurt myself, and when Hunter came to see if I'd broken my hand, his eyes, well… They told me."

"You're flirting again," Danielle's accusatory tone made Alex uncomfortable.

"I'm not flirting. I'm not doing anything."

"Do you ever stop?"

"What, Danielle? Being me? Talking? I didn't choose to be here, but I'm not going away. So no. I don't ever stop." Alex couldn't believe she'd gotten loud again, and neither could Little Sweetie who sat up, shaking on her lap. He looked at his bag as if he wanted to go hide and not come out until the grown-ups got their act together.

Alex's phone rang. "Hey, Willa. What's up?"

"Jerry said the server crashed."

"What's a server?"

"It has something to do with computers."

"How'd that happen?"

"Don't know."

"What am I supposed to do about it?"

Danielle gestured toward Alex. "He married her?"

"Ooh. I know," Alex said to Willa. "You know those nerdy boys who drive around in those Beetle cars painted red and white? Call and tell them that the server crashed. Have them send the best, Willa. Not some trainee. Fax everything to my e-mail. I want to know what they're charging before we agree to do business with them. Thanks, Willa. You did a good job."

"Thanks, Alex," she said and hung up.

Alex then turned to the woman she considered her archrival. "I'm not some brainiac like Renee, or a stunningly beautiful woman like you, Danielle. He married me because he wanted to have fun. And, honey, I'm a good time."

Little Sweetie yipped and Alex rubbed him. "I love you, too."

Renee sat down and pushed the rings down the table. "Hunter, would you look at my rings, too?"

He came and bent down beside Renee. "Will you feel any better knowing?"

After a moment, she shook her head.

"Then let it go until you go home. Get them appraised. This is too much for one day. You're right. It's time to go home."

"I hate him for this," Renee said. "But a part of me doesn't want to go back without him."

"I know how you feel." Alex walked gingerly on her weak knee. "You'll get better." She touched Renee's back and the woman began to sob.

Hunter soothed her too, offering reassurance and kindness.

Alex watched, unwilling to cry over Marc. He'd destroyed the last bit of fantasy in her life.

Tears streamed from Danielle's eyes and she dabbed them, her head on Tristan's shoulder.

Chris sat alone.

"Renee, do you want to come to my room and play in my makeup?" Alex offered.

Renee looked up and sucked up her tears. "Are you saying I need makeup?"

"No, but it's fun to have a girlfriend. Little Sweetie isn't much fun there, and I don't think Hunter's metrosexual."

The tension eased and Tristan and Danielle laughed.

"Definitely not," Hunter said.

"No, but thank you. I've never been invited to play makeup before."

"Oh, honey, we'll do a whole makeover. Cover up those red bumps on your cheeks, flatiron this big hair, a little concealer, then eye shadow and blush, you'll be good as new."

Renee looked at her hands. "I didn't know I needed so much work. Maybe another time. I think I'll go for a walk and maybe listen to the band in the lounge."

She wiped her tears with her hands.

"There's a great law firm in Atlanta named Lohan and Associates. I've never worked with them, but as a research librarian, I've heard great things about them. Just a suggestion." She then got up and hurried out.

"I'll check on her later," Chris said, standing and stretching.

"Come on," Alex said to Little Sweetie, patting his bag. The dog hopped inside.

"He's never going to know he's a dog if you treat him like he's a person," Danielle said.

"Exactly," Alex said. "My Little Sweetie deserves service with a smile, don't you?"

The dog barked his agreement.

"Chris, where's Marc's laptop? Was it destroyed in the crash?" Alex asked as she tried to decide whether she was hungry or not. The food Chris had bought hadn't been edible.

"Uh, I'm not sure."

"What about his briefcase?" Danielle asked. "I wonder what was in there? It might offer some insight as to why he was out here and why he lied to us."

"I have his briefcase," Chris said. "I can bring it over here tomorrow."

"Where do you live?" Tristan asked, waiting for Danielle to gather her papers.

"About twenty minutes from here. I have a one-bedroom condo."

Renee came rushing back. "I forgot my purse. No key to get into my room."

"You're not married?" Danielle asked Chris. Renee got her bag but seemed to wait to hear Chris's answer.

"No. No woman's been brave enough to stick around for my crazy schedule."

"You sound like Hunter," Alex said. "You guys need to learn how to compromise. Y'all are good looking, but you act like you're the last working men on earth." Alex waited at the door. "I'm not touching the door if there are men in the room."

"You're ridiculous," Danielle told her.

"My blood pressure is a hundred over seventy-eight. What's yours?" Alex shot back.

"A lot higher," Tristan added, and was rewarded with a dirty look from Danielle as he opened the door.

"Renee, Chris is bringing Marc's briefcase up here tomorrow so we can look at the contents," Alex told her as they walked to the elevator.

Renee held back after the others boarded. "I'm

going down first. I'll see you in the morning. Is nine o'clock okay?"

Alex, Danielle and Chris agreed. Each exited at their respective floor, though Chris followed Hunter off the elevator. "Can we talk?"

"I wasn't sure of Alex's plans," Hunter said, stopping at Alex's door.

"I'll be fine." Even to her own ears she sounded as if she didn't have a care in the world. "I've got a date, anyway, with my dog and my BlackBerry. See you tomorrow."

Closing the door, the smile fell from her face and she covered her mouth, the pain she'd been holding inside bubbling to the surface.

Her phone rang and she instinctively answered it. "Hello?"

"It's me, Willa."

"I know. What is it?"

"Your father is having the locks on the building changed."

"What's the name of the locksmith company?"

Willa gave it to her.

"You've been talking to Jerry?"

"Several times a day. He said you need to come home."

"I'll be back in two days. I'll call the locksmith

company and take care of everything. You've done a good job, Willa. I'm very proud of you. What about the cost of the server?"

"I faxed it. It's six hundred dollars."

Alex had no idea if that was good or not. "Pay him, but tell him to install software that tracks the keystrokes of every employee when they use the computers."

"Okay. You don't sound like you're feeling well. Do you want me to come out there?"

"No. I need you in Atlanta. I'll call you tomorrow."

"Okay, bye," Willa said and hung up.

Alex let the bag slip from her shoulder and Little Sweetie darted out and found a good hiding spot under the couch. He hated these days, she knew.

But there was nothing he or anyone could do for her.

When Alex started crying, nothing and no one could stop her until the pain was gone.

Chapter 7

"**Y**our brother was a piece of work. You want to explain why you thought it was a good idea for me to escort Alex out here?"

Chris sat down heavily. He looked older than the last time Hunter had seen him two years ago. Chris had been in Atlanta on business and had stopped by. He had understood Hunter's anger about the paralysis and had offered to help in any way possible, but Hunter had pushed him away.

He was glad Chris hadn't held it against him.

"I asked you to bring Alex because I didn't

think she'd come otherwise." He rubbed his eyes and sighed. "You got anything to drink in here?"

"No. Been off liquor for a while." Hunter didn't tell him since the heart surgery. There was only so much sympathy one person was allowed.

Chris eyed him carefully. "You in trouble?"

He patted his flat waist. "Fitness, man. Can't chase bad guys with baggage. They're getting younger."

Chris nodded, the caution gone. "You ain't lying. How about Danielle, Renee and Alex? They're a handful. Thank God for Tristan."

They both laughed.

Hunter rubbed his head. "I wouldn't want to meet Danielle on a really bad day. She could take down a wall. I thought she was going to beat Alex into the ground."

"You're right, but what about Alex. She's no shrinking violet."

"Chris, you should see her family. I'm surprised she's not in a psych ward. Her father's a bully, her brother's stealing from the family company and her grandmother bequeathed her controlling interest to the family fortune."

Eyes wide, Chris sat forward. "You've got to be kidding."

"No, dropped it in her lap. Now daddy and thieving brother are trying to wrest control from Alex, but she's fighting them. She had her brother arrested on her way out of Atlanta and she fired him. Get this, she's reading a book on how to become assertive. Given to her by your brother."

Chris's mouth fell open. "That's crazy. She called the judge like she's been a diva all her life."

"She's spoiled, but she was a powerless social-ite. Now she's pulling rank on everybody, and she doesn't realize there's a bitch hammer that usually goes along with being young, wealthy and powerful."

"Be glad," Chris said, resting his leg on the corner of the table. "You could have had a helluva trip from Atlanta."

"It was interesting, I'll give it that. Tell me about your brother." Hunter sat across from Chris in the leather extra grandé chair made for two. Since meeting Alexandria, he'd been eager to learn more about the man who'd captured Alex's heart.

"We weren't close because Marc never kept his word. He'd get angry with me for holding him accountable. I see why he distanced himself. He had too many secrets. Too many lies going on."

"Yeah, but he still dragged you into them. This is worse, leaving you to clean up his mess. He's still not accountable. I don't see how they didn't know."

"They're not trained to look at everything with different eyes like us. You saw them. They looked like refugees. Renee—"

Hunter waited for his friend to finish his sentence. Chris being conflicted over a woman was new. Chris was the type of man who always took care of business first. He closed his eyes for a minute and Hunter took the opportunity to order a pitcher of beer and chips from room service. He snagged a bottle of water from the refrigerator and drank.

"What about Renee?" Hunter opened the sliding glass door. Rain was still a ways off over the ocean, but the breeze it generated felt good against his skin. He just didn't get this kind of weather in Georgia.

"I thought she was going to have a nervous breakdown. She seemed so strong at the funeral, but at the meeting so fragile," Chris said.

"It's been a long day. She finds out her husband's dead by the brother-in-law she didn't know she had. She crosses the country and meets her husband's other wives. Then she finds out her marriage might not be real. Oh, and there's a good possibility her wedding rings are fake." Hunter shook his head sympathetically.

"All of that sounds bad. Let alone it being true."

Hunter answered the knock at the door and Tristan walked in. "I don't know about you guys, but I could use a drink."

Chris looked up at him. "Join the club. He just ordered a pitcher of beer and chips."

"I could cancel room service and we could hit the lounge downstairs," Hunter offered.

Tristan sat on the sofa opposite Chris. "Danielle's down there buying out the store. She needs some time alone. I saw Renee in the bar, so I got out of there. Where's Alex?"

"Probably made up like a clown in her room." Chris laughed at his joke, and Hunter gave him a dirty look.

"She's grieving, too. She found out her husband is really dead, wore the wrong dress to the funeral, brought her dog, got hollered at by Danielle, threatened by Renee, and she fell down. She's had a bad day."

"My brother was a jerk."

Another knock sent Hunter to the door. He

accepted the food and drinks and the waiter nodded to Chris. "Good evening, Mr. Foster. Is everything to your guests' liking?"

"Yes, Daniel, I believe it is."

"Can I bring you anything else? We have finger foods like wings and crab cakes. Or you might like a heartier meal."

Chris smiled at the man, took the check from Hunter and signed it. "This is good for now. We'll probably end up in the Diamond lounge a little later."

"Good deal," the young waiter said. "Good evening, gentlemen." He then exited with the serving tray.

Tristan gave a nod of approval. "Talk about service with a smile."

"Yeah," Chris said, accepting a glass of beer from Hunter. "He's hungry, and I like that about him."

"You own this place, don't you?" Hunter asked him.

Chris asked. "Only sixty percent."

"Congratulations." Hunter shook Chris's hand.

Tristan did too. "Too bad all they're going to remember is coming here to bury their husband."

Chris threw up his hands. "I'm not apologizing for him anymore. I don't know what made him do what he did."

"Don't you want to know?" Hunter asked.

"At first I thought I didn't. But, yeah. How in the hell did Marc think he could get away with this? I mean, he was a good-looking guy, but he was no model. Our father was a decent-looking dude, but why did he think he deserved three women?"

"Three gorgeous women," Hunter added.

"That has nothing to do with a man's mind that marries three women," Tristan told them, leaning back, beer in hand.

"What is it then?"

"He was a confidence man. These women were insecure in an area of their lives, and Marc addressed a need they couldn't fill on their own. He in turn took something from them. That's what con men do."

"Alexandria flew out here believing he wasn't really dead," Hunter said and sipped his water.

Both men winced.

"So, what's your relationship to Danielle?" Hunter asked Tristan.

"We're business partners. Her brother was my best friend. He was killed in the Iraq war."

"I'm sorry," Hunter said.

"Me, too," Chris added.

"Thank you," Tristan said. "After Dani stopped modeling she was looking for an investment and we decided she'd buy out her brother's portion of the business. We've been partners ever since."

"Nothing else?" Chris asked, looking at Tristan closely.

"No," he answered the question without pause. But there was something there. Hunter couldn't say that the look in Tristan's eyes was that of more than a friend. It was a hunch that he felt more for Danielle, but he felt more for Alex, and he'd only known her for two days.

"Do you want to check on Alex?" Chris asked.

Hunter looked at the closed connecting door. He'd done it at least ten times in the past half hour. "I figured she needed some time alone. I told her I'd stay a couple extra days, then head back to Atlanta."

Even as he said this, he and Tristan walked to the door.

"Man, I think she's crying." Taller than Hunter's six feet by two inches, Tristan nodded. "She is. Go see if you can help her. I'm going to check on Danielle and Renee. They all might be breaking down. Chris, I'll check with you later."

Chris got up, too. "You take care of Danielle. I'll see about Renee. Hit my cell if you need anything." He gave the number to Tristan and they left together.

Hunter knocked on the door and let himself in.

The blinds had been closed, the sheer curtains drawn around the bed. Alex lay in the middle, the thick comforter pulled back, the sheet covering her legs and hips.

"Hunter, is that you?" Her voice was full of tears.

"Yeah. What's going on?"

"Don't look at me. I'm just feeling sorry for myself. I'll be okay."

He pulled the white sheer panel back and stepped up on the platform to sit on the bed. "You don't have to grieve alone."

She drew in a watery breath. "Yes, I do."

"No, you don't."

"Yes, I do. I'm, like, the biggest loser here." She started crying again and fumbled for something.

"What are you doing?" he asked.

"Getting a fresh towel."

"You have a crying towel?"

"More than one."

"I can't see. I have to turn on the light."

"No! I look hideous when I cry. You can't turn

on the light. You can't." She started winding up, her body shaking and he rubbed her arm and back.

"Okay. Okay," he soothed. "Can I open the blinds just a little? There's a half moon and it won't allow too much light. I just want to make sure you're okay, and then I'll go."

"Okay."

Light from the moon reflected off the gold-trimmed accessories and austere finish of the room, and Hunter was glad the guys had convinced him to come over. He poured her a glass of water and sat close.

"Come here, sweetheart. I want you to drink this."

"You don't have to take care of me. I have to learn how to be independent." Even as she said the words her chest shook. Her hair was all over her head and she wiped the curls to one side.

She was wrapped around a pillow, her face pressed into a thick washcloth.

He immediately knew what her problem was. "Come here," he coaxed, tugging on her arm. "Did you know that part of being independent is knowing when to ask for help?"

He stroked her back, noting that her pajamas were a silk camisole and shorts. "Come on."

Alex finally sat up, took the glass and drained it.

"Now I'll have more tears. I was taught to never cry in front of people."

"I see." He brushed her tears away with his thumb. "Well, I'm not people. I'm your friend and you can cry in front of me anytime you want."

"Do you cry, Hunter?" She wiped her eyes with her cloth.

"Sure."

"You do?" Her voice brushed at the darkness. "When was the last time?"

"When my arm was paralyzed and I didn't think I'd ever be able to use it again. All I could think about was all I hadn't done."

"What hadn't you done?"

"Played the saxophone. Run with the bulls in Barcelona. Cheered at a Super Bowl. Built my house. Carried my bride across the threshold."

She sniffed and put her chin on her knees. "You could put her on your back."

Hunter laughed. "I hadn't thought of that."

"Do you really want to do all those things?"

"Yep, I do."

"You will."

"I know." He pushed her hair over her shoulder. "Do you feel better?"

"Some. Will you lie down with me? I don't want to be alone tonight."

"I can't, Alexandria." Two big tears rolled down her cheeks. "Come on. Why the tears?"

"Why won't you?"

"Because you're in a lot of pain and I don't want you to wake up tomorrow and question your judgment today."

She shook her head. "I don't have anyone else but you. Even my dog is hiding from me. I promise. No regrets. I need to feel your heartbeat to know that I'm alive, or I won't make it. I've been alone too long. I feel invisible. I need to know that I'm here." She pulled him, but Hunter resisted.

Alex cried as she leaned over the side of the bed, trying to untie his shoes. "Take these off. Please."

He grabbed her shoulders and brought her back up on the bed. "Alex, stop."

Her startled expression crumpled. "Just leave me alone. Didn't I say that from the beginning? I didn't ask you to come in here. You've made me feel like a fool all over again. Just get out!" She struggled to get away from him.

"Get out!"

"No. Stop. Lie down." He couldn't leave her. He wouldn't.

"He didn't love me. Don't do this to me. Not you, too. Please, Hunter," she cried, and something in him broke.

"Okay." He pulled her into his lap and rocked her.

"I'm so stupid."

"You could never be stupid," he said, wishing he could kill Marc all over again.

"He took advantage of me."

"Yes, he did. He was a confidence man."

"What's that?" She sat up for a second and he considered moving her off his lap for his own good.

"A con man. A man who preys on vulnerable women."

"He could have tricked anyone?" She curled into him and pulled the blanket with her.

"Yes, sweetheart," he said, rocking her.

"I still don't feel better," she said, her body shaking with tears and shame.

"You have to stop crying or you'll get sick. Come on, lie down. Shh," he said, wishing her big sobs would stop. Hunter covered her completely with the sheet and comforter.

"Where are you going?" she asked, hiccupping.

"I need to have my cell phone on me. I'll be right back." He darted into his room for his blanket and phone.

Before reaching the bed he turned up the air conditioner. He needed every reason for her to stay under the covers and for him to stay on top of them.

Hunter removed his shoes and climbed on top of the bed fully dressed, lying down behind her.

"I can't feel you," she complained, lying on her side.

"You want it all, don't you?"

"Yes," she said in a small voice.

"Scoot back." Alex moved back and Hunter wrapped his arms around her as much as he could with the comforter between them. "Better?"

"Some," she said.

This was still too much for him given that she'd just lost her husband. But what could he do? Leave her to cry all night alone? Holding her a while ago had made him feel things he hadn't in a long time.

Alex was a woman he could want and he'd never had more inappropriate thoughts before in his life.

"What brought all this crying on?" he asked, inhaling the aroma of strawberry shampoo.

"I was thinking about why Marc would still be married to those two. We're all so different. Maybe it was the sex. Maybe they're better at it than me. I know I'm not that experienced, but they don't look like they're experts, either."

He didn't think she had anything to worry about in that area, but he couldn't reassure her without sounding like a pervert. "It might not be that."

"Maybe Marc was playing games with my head or maybe he was just using me. The more I think about our relationship, the more I want to cry. Marc is like all the other men in my life. He betrayed me."

"Don't blame yourself for his failings. You can look for answers in a thousand places and never know why Marc did what he did."

"I feel incomplete. I have to know. I thought he loved me. These last few months, I felt like he didn't."

"Why do you say that?"

"He stopped making love to me."

Hunter leaned up. He'd known Alex for two days. The woman oozed sex appeal. He was spooning her right now, thinking about whales so he wouldn't get a hard-on, and her husband wouldn't make love to her? If it hadn't been proven already, it was now. The man had been crazy. "How long had it been?"

"Six months."

"Half your marriage?" he asked indignantly.

"Yes," she said, reaching for her towel.

Hunter regretted making so much of her

celibate marriage. "I'm sorry, Alex. I shouldn't sound shocked. I'm not judging you."

"Don't worry. Maybe if I'd been better, he'd have gotten rid of those extra wives." She started crying again.

"That's not true."

"You don't know, Hunter," she choked.

"You're right, I don't. But, Alex, it isn't about sex."

"Then it doesn't make sense. I try to stay attractive, but it's obvious they're smarter than me, and—"

"Come on, don't put yourself down."

"I'm not. I'm just facing facts. If he was going to marry me, he should have divorced them. I'm a fool," she said and cried.

"You're a victim." Hunter smoothed her hair and caressed the contour of her ear. Everything about her was just right. How could he express that there was more right with her than wrong? That if he were Marc, he wouldn't have had to choose from three, she would have been the one. He was jaded, he knew.

He didn't know much of anything about her. It was dark, they were in an emotional situation, and he wasn't going to start being logical until he was back in Atlanta under normal circumstances. "You're going to be all right."

"Do you promise?" she asked.

"Yes, I do. Now go to sleep."

"Good night, Hunter."

"Good night."

Hunter closed his eyes and felt himself falling asleep. The bed shook and he heard Little Sweetie's doggie tags.

"Chicken," he said, and felt the dog lie down behind his back.

Quiet descended and Alex snuggled closer.

She sniffed every so often and Hunter rubbed her back through the blanket. He was glad for the barrier because had it not been there, he'd have followed more primal instincts to make her feel better.

Hunter fell asleep and dreamed he was whale watching. His dream shifted and Alex was next to him. When she turned over, they were body to body.

"You asleep?" she asked in the fog of his dream.

"Mmm-hmm," he said as her hair caressed his arm.

Hunter heard himself snore, and realized he was somewhere between dreaming and awake. "Do you think he loved me?" she asked.

"I don't know, sweetheart."

Whales arched out of the water, their large bodies crashing back into the sea.

"I'm being punished."

"Why?" he asked her, feeling her skin beneath his palm.

"Because I wasn't in love with him anymore."

Hunter's eyes flew open.

Dawn had broken through the blinds, showing off gray and overcast skies. He lifted his head from her chest, his mouth a breath away from the caramel tip of her nipple.

Alex was flat on her back against him, her heart beating against his palm.

Hunter stole from her bed, knowing if he didn't leave then, he'd claim her, the unmarried woman that she was, and help her erase every memory she had of the husband who hadn't deserved her.

Chapter 8

Alex stared at the contents of Marc's steel brief-case, the one she'd seen him carry dozens of times. Only now she wasn't watching it crash to the foyer floor as she had when she'd seduced him when he'd walked into their home on the eve of his thirty-fourth birthday.

Or the time she used it as a pedestal and invited him to investigate the finer details of her Brazilian wax, with his tongue, from behind.

Or the last time she'd seen him when she'd stared at the case with disdain, wondering what was so interesting at his job that could keep him gone from his bride for weeks at a time.

Now she knew.

Her earlier thoughts of lovemaking caused her body to throb, and the feelings pulsed all the way to her head.

Alex tried to banish the thoughts with the heel of her hand on her forehead.

Renee sat beside her in the chair, dressed in beige no-wrinkle pants, a white shirt and a red vest. Alex didn't want to tell her she was a fashion emergency, because her makeup was pretty and her earrings were stylish.

"What are you doing?" Renee asked.

"Thinking," Alex explained.

"It takes all that?" Danielle asked.

Sitting across the table from them, Danielle posed in the latest jeans and designer top. Yet, she seemed even more unhappy today than yesterday. The woman was practically a commercial for antidepressants.

"I see Cruella Danielle is back, and I was hoping for Mary Poppins Danielle. I hope the guys get back with breakfast soon. Maybe coffee will put you in a better mood."

"This isn't a game." Danielle stalked around the table as if it were a runway.

"Who thinks it is?" Alex felt the need to confront her. Danielle acted as if she was the only one with feelings. "Do you think just because you were married to Marc the longest that gives you the right to be the angriest?"

"As a matter of fact I do."

A tension headache from too much crying pulled at her eyes, and she stared at Danielle, who looked as if she hadn't slept well either. But that didn't give her the automatic right to be nasty.

"That's irrational," Renee chimed in. "I couldn't sleep for thinking about this debacle. The ramifications are far-reaching, ladies. I'm not sure what I'll say to my friends."

"I could care less about them. I care about what this will do to my image professionally."

"Please," Alex scoffed. "You're in the package-delivery business. Nobody even sees you. Image might have been everything when you were modeling, but not now. This is a blow to your little ego," she said, drawing a circle in the air around Danielle.

"You need to watch your mouth, little girl." Danielle took a step back.

"Yeah, be quiet, Alex," Renee warned.

"No. She's not the queen bee." Alex faced Danielle, her hand on her hip. "I know it's hard facing your competition, but at least now you know what you can do better the next time."

Before she finished the word, Danielle slapped her.

Alex screamed and Renee got between them, pointing Danielle into a seat and guiding Alex to the other end of the table.

"What is wrong with you people? *Violence?*" Renee yelled. "Are you from the streets? I can't believe this."

"I've never been hit before," Alex cried, holding her cheek.

Renee moved Alex's hand gingerly and examined her cheek. "You're okay." She walked away, holding her forehead. "I can't believe you hit her."

"Maybe she'll should stop running her mouth," Danielle retorted.

"I'm sorry, Alex," Renee said, "but you had it coming. That was mean."

"What? Why?" Alex's eyes stung with unshed tears.

"You're young and you've got a nice body.

You've got money, and well, you walked into your husband's funeral wearing a white polka-dot dress with toile, and come-do-me pumps. You brought your dog like it was a pet store. You have pretty hair," Renee said with a sad shake of her head. "You make people want to hit you. I'm sorry, but it's true."

Renee slid onto the table and swung her legs, folding her hands. She looked over her shoulder. "Danielle, people want to hit you, too. At least I do."

Alex looked past Renee to Danielle. Despite having been the aggressor, she looked shaken as well. She walked over and sat on the other side of Renee. She stuck out her hand to Alex, who leaned away.

"What's that for?" Alex asked.

"So you can hit me back."

"I'm like Dr. King. A passive resister. Hunter told me that. I'm a lover not a fighter."

"I don't think you should drag Dr. King's name through all of this," Renee advised.

Alex shrugged. "You're probably right."

Danielle looked chastised. "I shouldn't have done that. I'm sorry. I'm stressed out. I can't believe I'm hearing this. It's been a nightmare from the first phone call. But that's no excuse."

The silence was thick and heavy. "Why do you want to hit me, Renee?"

"Like she said, you're gorgeous, but you've got a chip on your shoulder the size of Stone Mountain. You were married to Marc first, but you act like we secretly knew he was married to you."

"I don't know that you didn't."

"And that's why. You know, in my real life, I don't cross paths with women like you. Former models, like you, Danielle, and rich women who are like you, Alex. I work with academics. We wash our face with bar soap and read dusty journals. I get excited when my friends are nominated for Pulitzer Prizes, and I keep track of which of them is nominated for the Nobel Prize. I don't have affairs with married men."

"Neither do I," Alex added.

"I felt like I'd won a Pulitzer when Marc found me. So to be treated as if I'm less than honorable is degrading especially when I didn't ever think I'd find someone in the first place."

"What about all those professors?" Danielle asked. "I would think you wouldn't have a problem finding a smart man in the academic world."

Renee's face squeezed for a second and she played with the hem of her vest.

"They bored you to tears, didn't they?" Alex said. "I always thought professors were yawners."

Renee smiled and the other two laughed. "Some are nice, but most are married. I wanted to find someone outside of academia. But to our original topic, I didn't know, Danielle."

"Well, how do you think it makes me feel to see that he's married not only an intelligent librarian, but a rich socialite? I wasn't good enough, so he was auditioning my replacements."

Startled, Alex and Renee shared a moment before looking at Danielle.

"That's not true," Alex told her. "Hunter said he was a confidence man, a con man. Marc tricked us, ladies. And he wanted something from all of us."

"Tristan said the same thing."

"So did Chris," Renee added.

The women eyed each other, gauging whether they should trust one other.

The men walked in bearing coffee and breakfast foods.

Hunter took one look at Alex and headed straight for her. He caressed her cheek, his breath and his fingers giving the same feeling of intimacy against her skin. "What happened to you?"

"Danielle hit me. I'm okay. We had a talk. She offered for me to hit her back."

"Is that right?" Tristan said, sitting by Danielle. "Why'd you do that?"

"She called me Cruella Danielle."

Tristan shook his head and rubbed the back of her neck. Danielle looked sorry as she rubbed her temple right by her eyes.

"I said we were her competition, and she should pay attention to what we're doing so she'll get it right the next time, and she hit me. I deserved it," Alex went on. "Anyway, I'm going back to Atlanta. We can go with the law firm Renee suggested or another if you all would like. I thought I'd like California, but not so much, now that I've been here."

Alex picked up Little Sweetie who'd been hiding under the table.

Chris put the coffee in front of Renee and Alex. "Please eat before you go."

"No, thank you. I just want to go home and start a new life."

"Try, Alex. It's a long flight to Atlanta and as hard as they try, airline food isn't the best."

"Maybe a bite of bagel." She sat down, studying the briefcase. "Where are the folders?

Marc always had green and blue folders." She picked at a boiled egg, giving Little Sweetie a piece. Hunter sat a chair away and patted his leg. Little Sweetie hopped over and cuddled on his lap.

"I never saw any folders," Danielle replied, narrowing her eyes at Alex.

"These are my house keys." Renee slid the ring through her fingers.

Chris walked around the table. "Alex is right. There were green and blue folders, but they were related to his job and were returned to the company a few days ago."

"What did Marc do?" Alex asked. "I never understood that."

"He sold plastic," Renee said. "Tarps of all shapes, sizes and colors to the government." Everyone looked at her. "Is that another lie?" she asked tentatively.

"No, but it just sounds strange, like that's all he did," Danielle said. "He sold large plastic containers the government used for storage of other goods. But why am I speaking up for him? He's a lout. A dead one. Chris, can you give us more details on how he died?" Danielle asked. "You said his plane crashed, but there was nothing in the newspaper, and I still don't know why he was out here. What happened?"

Tristan made no secret of holding Danielle's hand.

"Well, he'd flown down from a few days in Marina del Rey. Marc was landing and the plane skidded off the runway and crashed. Ultimately, the cause of death was listed as choking to death."

"Choking to death." Renee rose. "How's that possible? Was he eating? Was there smoke? I didn't know the plane burned."

"It didn't. He choked on an apparatus," Chris said evasively.

"What aren't you saying?" Hunter asked. "They've come all this way to find out about their husband and you're holding something back."

"He choked on a wedding ring."

The women looked at one another. "What?"

"Whose wedding ring?" Danielle asked.

"Does it matter?" Chris walked to the window and back. "We have a lot more important matters to deal with, like Marc's life insurance policies, and the liability each of you faces for having been married to the same man." He gave each of them an envelope. "That's a copy of the death certificate. You're going to need it."

"Thanks. Two of us unwittingly committed fraud." Shock rippled Renee's voice. "And we could face criminal charges."

Alex put the envelope in her back pocket and pulled her vibrating phone from her side. "Hello?" she turned away from Danielle's disapproving frown and walked into the hallway. "Hi, Mr. Feinstein."

"You asked me to call if there were any problems and there are. When will you be home?"

"Tomorrow. What's going on?"

"There are large discrepancies in your personal and business accounts that don't balance with what your auditors are finding."

"What types of discrepancies?"

"Large withdrawals, Mrs. Wright-Foster. Money was moved over the past six months and not accounted for."

"Who took it? Just tell me."

"We can talk when you get home, Mrs. Wright-Foster."

"No, tell me now." She clenched her jaw and then let it go. She was before the firing squad. Bracing herself wouldn't stop the sting of the bullets.

"Some of the withdrawals were allegedly

made by you, but the signatures don't match. The others were very obviously made by Mr. Foster. We'll have a complete report for you tomorrow. Let's say four-thirty?"

"Four-thirty is fine. Goodbye." She held the phone to her chest. *Marc, you stole from me, too? What else can you do to humiliate me?* Renee had said those words yesterday and now Alex heard herself saying them.

Her phone rang and Alex saw that it was Willa. For the first time since taking over the leadership of Wright Enterprises, Alex sent the call to voice mail.

Chapter 9

Hunter sat in his office reviewing the e-file of the newest clients his company was providing security for. This was a level-one security plan. Business executives from the fashion industry were planning their semiannual board meeting in Nova Scotia and needed to be moved from New York and back without incident.

His team was to make sure the six men were safe, and that everything went smoothly. Meaning, word of any dalliances that might take place didn't reach home base.

Hunter reread the files on each man and committed them to memory. He then assigned a security specialist who would oversee the project, then e-mailed the assignment with detailed instructions.

The project leader, Samia, called immediately. "Hunter, welcome back."

"I've been back for two weeks, Sam, but you were gone. How's it going?"

"Fine. I can't believe you're giving me this big of a project. Usually I get kids." Samia's toothy grin hid her fierce talent. She spoke six languages, and was a martial-arts expert in tae kwon do, akido, capoeira, sumo and kendo.

"I give you children because you're good at predicting the unpredictable."

"That's cool, I appreciate the promotion. I see a problem with only one of the clients. He's got a substance-abuse problem."

"Active?" Hunter asked, looking through the file and locating the client.

"Yes. They're not known for that in Nova Scotia, which means he'll be trying to import, which means trouble for everyone," they said together.

"I'll make the necessary call. He might not be going," Hunter finished.

"That may be a Health Insurance Portability and Accountability Act, a HIPPA issue," Samia cautioned, "discussing his medical history with his boss."

"No worries there. He signed a release so I could review his file, but I'm not going to his boss. I'll be talking directly to him. I'll outline the penalty for importing drugs, the company's policy on arrest in a foreign country and the length of incarceration for said arrest. If he decides to go, he'll be searched, thoroughly. He may decide to stay home on his own."

"Excellent. And if something should happen should he decide to go?"

"He'll have all the information he'll need to contact the State Department."

Hunter's cell phone rang and he saw that it was Alex. "I've got to go, Sam. Call me later if you have any questions."

"I've got this. Thanks."

The phone rang again and excitement coursed through him. They'd been home for two weeks and with the exception of two short conversations, they hadn't talked extensively or seen each other.

He'd wanted to give her some time, himself too, but that didn't mean he hadn't thought about her every hour of every day. He'd already decided that if he hadn't heard from her by noon today, he'd drop by her office and see how things were going. She'd beat him by thirty minutes.

"Good morning," he said, knowing his day had taken a turn for the better.

"Hunter, it's so good to hear your voice. It seems like forever. Have you got a few minutes?"

"Sure. What's up?"

"For lunch, I mean."

He looked at his watch. It was almost time for lunch.

"Well, Hunter, can I buy you lunch?"

He eyed his gym bag and the list of weights he was supposed to be doing to keep his arm strong. "Sure. Where and when?"

"I'm in your reception area now. Are you too busy for me to steal you away right now?"

"No." He pressed a button on his computer and saw her in the lobby. She looked gorgeous, and more like a coed than a grown woman. Still, she appealed to the man in him like no other.

"Give me a minute. I'll be right out."

"Thanks. Bye."

Hunter hurried into his bathroom and brushed his teeth. Dabbed on cologne and checked his face and hair. He wasn't sure why he was nervous, but he wanted to be at his best when he saw her.

Back in his office, he took a few deep breaths and popped in a breath mint, then realized his error when the flavors blended.

He spit the mint out and straightened his shirt, wondering why he was nervous for a woman he wasn't even dating.

Because he wanted to make more than a good impression. He wanted to date her.

Truthfully he wanted more than that, but for now, lunch was going to have to be good enough.

He headed out his office and down the hallway, his staff efficient and quiet. Most worked in the field, but a few floated around, often following up on reports with their teams, but their jobs weren't the type where they had to report in every day to a desk, to sit and wait for assignments. A lot of times the sitting and waiting took place in cars or restaurants doing surveillance.

He saw Alex before she saw him, and he was surprised at her weight loss. He'd held her all night long and had become acquainted with the gentle curves of her body, and he could tell she'd shed a lot of weight.

She was in four-inch heels, a black skirt that was so tight it ought to have been against the law, and a red top that crisscrossed her body and was tied in the back. Her hair was in a bun with ringlets cascading in careless droplets over her shoulders, and she didn't have Little Sweetie.

Hunter took a deep breath and before he could let it out, Alex pivoted.

"Hunter," she said, looking distracted as she approached and hugged him. He held her for a long time.

"Why does it seem like a lifetime since I last saw you?"

He looked her over from head to toe and enjoyed the scent of strawberry shampoo and perfume. "I don't know." He ran his hand over her hair, looking deeply into her eyes. "You don't look like you're feeling well."

She hadn't completely released him, so he kept his arm around her waist. "I don't, but that's beside the point. I need you," she said, tilting her head sideways. She caressed his arm until their palms met and held.

His receptionist, Twyla, had been with him for a year and had seen lots of things, but she'd never seen anyone hug him then lead him to his office. Her eyebrow was arched. He couldn't stop smiling. Neither could she.

"Hunter, I really need you," Alex said again

as soon as the door closed. He wished she'd ended the sentence in his bed nude, because that's how his dreams ended each morning when he awoke.

"First tell me how you've been." He took his seat behind his desk, hoping she'd take the chair opposite him so he could focus.

She dropped a black bag on the floor by the desk.

"I've been okay. I came back to the locks changed on the doors of the building and my father trying to take over the company. The employees are stressed and confused, and I'm distracted with Marc and my life. But the situation with work was an easy fix."

"That doesn't sound easy."

"I had my brother arrested again. I'd fired him, but he didn't take that seriously."

"What's with the power play?"

"It's ridiculous, I know, but power is the only thing my brother and my dad understand. Having him rearrested wasn't without a good reason, Hunter." Alex walked over to the window overlooking the gardens of Cobb Manor Industrial Park.

"My brother had collected some of the money from clients and hadn't turned it in to the accountant like he should have. Since he'd been arrested on the embezzling charge, he was arrested for theft again. He was so angry at me, he admitted to the arresting officer that he wasn't giving me anything—meaning he wasn't going to turn in the money until I quit. Naturally, they didn't need to hear more than that." Her shrug reflected the helplessness in her voice.

Hunter shook his head. "He's not too bright, is he?"

"No, and he has a business degree that my father raves about."

"Why do you look as if you feel guilty?"

"I set him up. I shouldn't have told my father to collect the money. I wanted to make them responsible."

"Alex, that's Mervyn's fault. There may have been a better way to go about getting the money, but making them responsible is the only way to get people to grow up. Your intentions were in the right place. How can I help you?"

Hunter's phone rang. "Just a moment. Hunter," he answered.

Alex turned to the garden and seemed to become absorbed in the beauty of the blooming flowers, as he often did.

When he'd chosen the location the gardens

hadn't been complete, but now that they were done, he couldn't imagine being anywhere else.

He watched her back and shoulder muscles to see if the hypnotic beauty had the desired effect on her.

She didn't move even when he finished his call and came up behind her. He held back, now that she had finally found some semblance of peace.

A fawn had emerged from the bushes across from them, and Alex's breath caught as the doe stepped through seconds later. Mother and child gazed at them, then cut through the trees ten yards down.

Alex's shoulders rose high with tension and stress and she took a deep breath and held it, then exhaled through pursed lips he could see through the reflected glass. "That was beautiful."

She turned around and didn't seem surprised to see him standing behind her. "I've missed you, Hunter. I've missed talking to you and being with you. There's so much I want to tell you, but the most important thing is that I need you."

Her bedtime confession rested heavily on his mind, especially since he wasn't completely sure Alex knew she'd made it. She'd been emotional and possibly asleep when she'd uttered that she hadn't loved her husband.

A breeze from the east ruffled the chrysanthemums, but he cared nothing for the breeze and everything for how tenderly Alex held his hand as she walked back to his desk.

Hunter took control and waited until she was seated before letting go and taking his seat.

"Tell me what's going on," he said, leaning back in his chair. "Have you heard from Renee or Danielle?"

"After you verified that the law firm Renee recommended was legit, I sent my paperwork in. That was two weeks ago. They said it could be weeks or months before we hear something."

"Why so long?"

"Marc and I were married in the Bahamas. Their records are harder to verify over the phone and fax, so the attorney had to go down there. They may have to interview the judge or clerk of the court. I'm not sure. Anyway, all I know is that there's a discrepancy."

Alex looked down, her face lined with anxiety. Hunter almost went to her, but he held himself back. He considered the characteristics he needed in a woman, and Alex didn't have them. He needed someone older and established, and busy. He needed someone who didn't need him.

In some ways he thought of her as still married, although the status was questionable.

"Even if there's a discrepancy, that doesn't mean it isn't going to go in your favor."

"There wouldn't be a discrepancy then, Hunter. I'm not that dumb. I'm sorry," she said quickly before he could jump all over her.

She rubbed her eyes then cupped her cheeks. "I know I'm not dumb. I know I told you I want you to lie to me, but I don't. I want the truth. No matter how harsh. Living on fools' island landed me where I am today. That's why I need your expertise. Two weeks ago the accountants found evidence that Marc was stealing from me. Not just me, but the company. If you add in the fact that my brother was stealing, and my father collected money from those companies and is refusing to turn it over, well, I've landed Wright Enterprises in a very bad position."

Hunter went to Alex and sat in the other visitor's chair. She rubbed her eyes again. "I'm at a loss about what to do," she said, her legs pressed together, her hands folded.

"I'm trying to hold on. I've read my book on being assertive. I've got that down," she said, looking him in the eye.

"You're doing quite well." He shifted under her gaze, knowing she wasn't aware of the power of her sex appeal. She was having a crisis and he needed to stay focused. She pulled her bag from the side of his desk.

"I bought another book on being the best CEO you can be. How top employees succeed. How to motivate successful people." She stacked the books as she read the titles. "How to sell in five minutes. Play to win. Close the sale. Turn nos into yeses. Big fish, tiny bowl. Knock 'em dead with professional appeal. This book is about sex appeal, Hunter. It was kind of nasty, to be honest."

He kept quiet in the face of her near breakdown. She shoved all the books back in the bag and began to pull at the shirt she was wearing. "I even went to a seminar on dressing for success. But being all bound up in these clothes makes me feel like a dominatrix."

Hunter laughed. "Sweetheart, you don't have to dress that way."

"The seminar leader said dress for success in a power suit. This has a jacket. But I feel like a mummy," she said, pulling at the ties on the back of her shirt. "It's like a corset."

He couldn't help himself, and laughed again.

"It's not funny… My hair is so…tight." She tried to run her fingers through it but got nowhere. "It's driving me crazy. I haven't brought my dog to work, and I miss him, Hunter. I'm so stressed out, I feel like I'm in my thirties. I really want to get out of all of this."

She started pulling at the collar of her top, and for the first time he saw that her crisis was real.

"Whoa. What are you doing?"

"I have to take this off."

"And do what?" he asked her.

"You have a T-shirt. Don't you?"

He looked around as she struggled with the buttons, intermittently shaking her hands. "In my gym bag."

"Well." It was more a statement than a question. Her diva horns were emerging, but Hunter still thought she wasn't bad.

She pulled at the ties on her shirt. "Hunter, I'm going crazy. I'm twenty-three, and I've got the chance to prove I'm not a loser to my whole family, and I feel like my dead husband is flushing my life down the toilet. Help me get this off!"

"Wait." He guided her into his bathroom where he flipped on the light and stood her in front of the mirror. "Slow down," he advised.

He wrestled with the tiny knot the tip of the shirt had been tied into. "Who did this?"

"Willa," she said, fanning her face. "She lives with me now. I hate my hair like this." Alex started pulling bobby pins from the bun, tossing them into the garbage can. He loved her hair. It uncoiled like a snake with each pin that she removed.

Hunter finally gave up and pulled the shirt, ripping the ends. "I don't care," she said, wiggling.

"What does Marc have to do with this?"

"He stole money from the company. I'll look like a fool if I don't find it and put that money back. They'll crucify me, Hunter, and I'll never be able to redeem myself to my family."

He met her gaze in the mirror and his heart twisted. She looked so lost and sad.

"Stop thinking for five minutes, okay?" he asked.

"Okay."

He pushed her head down and took over pulling out the pins until her hair was as free as her body from the shirt.

Being with her half dressed in his bathroom felt so normal. Hunter thought of how easily it would be to get used to it. He sent his fingers through her hair and caressed her scalp. Her head fell forward, and he couldn't help but think of how if he had his way, he'd love to take her home and massage all of her. "Better?"

"Yes, that feels better. What's happening to me?" She'd never been this vulnerable before. All Hunter knew was that if she was his, he'd never make her feel insecure and unstable.

"Anxiety attack, that's all. You're going to have to practice staying calm."

"How can I when I feel as if the world is coming apart under my feet?"

"It's not, Alex."

"I know. I've got to be strong." She stood a little straighter. "I've never had an anxiety attack before. Can you massage my shoulders too, please," she said when he started to pull away.

"Alex, this is dangerous territory."

"For me too, Hunter." Her voice seduced him, even though her gaze said she knew exactly what she was doing.

"Really? How?" He kneaded her left shoulder and down her arm, then down her right, wanting to plant his lips down her back.

"I'm a physical person, and I like how your hands feel on me. I need to touch, and I need be touched, but I understand. I shouldn't tempt you if I can't deliver."

She rubbed her temples with the heel of her hand.

"Don't get all wound up again. It's not that I'm not attracted to you, Alex, I am." Hunter couldn't resist caressing her arms and shoulders.

"You are?"

"Yes, I am."

"Well, I'm glad to know that. But I need to know that I'm desired. It's been over six months since I've been made love to. When I got married, I got used to doing what grown-ups do. That whole body-to-body, sex-to-sex thing. When we were in California, I couldn't sleep until I was right beside you."

"I wondered how that happened," he said, half joking.

"I needed to feel your arms around me, not that mountain of blankets you were trying to suffocate me under."

He smiled at her through the mirror. "I don't think you know how sexy you are." He had a bird's-eye view of her through the mirror in her sexy, lace bra and from the back with the cutest curve of her bottom over the baddest "fuck-me-pumps" he'd ever seen.

He didn't know what dress-for-success book she'd been reading, but every woman needed to have one if this was the end result. Hunter stepped out of the bathroom and grabbed the T-shirt from his gym bag. Alex pulled it over her head and tied it on the side.

She went and sat on the sofa and crossed her legs, waiting for him to join her.

"I used to know I was sexy, but my husband stopped making love to me, and to find out that he was making love to two other women, well, my confidence is in the garbage."

"You're a beautiful woman, Alex. You won't have a problem finding someone."

"I'm not worried. I didn't come here specifically to seduce you. I came here for your help and I pretended that I was going to take you to lunch. If you want I'll still feed you."

"I'm not hungry."

"But I need you in more ways than one, Hunter."

"Lay it out for me."

"I need you to help me find the money Marc stole from the company so I can put it back. And I need you to be my bodyguard. I don't trust my family."

"Do you feel as if you're in danger?"

"I feel as if my father and brother would do a whole lot to get what they want. What that is, I don't know. I'm not crying wolf."

She went to her bag and pulled out a piece of colored paper. "I received this note today. It basically says leave the company or I'll regret it."

"Put it on the table for me."

Alex set it down and Hunter handled it carefully, reading it. The script was thin and looping, taking up the top half of the page. "Have you seen this stationery before?"

"No. It's not something I'd use at work."

"Do you think someone in your family would really try to hurt you?"

"My brother's been in jail twice and according to him, I'm the cause. Possibly," she said, and her eyes filled with tears. Hunter knew he'd help her. He hated to see women cry.

"I'll work with you. Nobody will hurt you."

"Nine to five?" she asked.

"Yes," he said. "But I can't be with you intimately. Mixing the two is bad business."

"That's where you're wrong, Hunter. We're already in the same place emotionally. Did you know that butterflies only live for about three weeks?"

He smiled at her, wondering where she was going. "Really? Why would I need to know that?"

"Since I got back, I've been in my office from

sunup to sundown, and every day I see this pretty yellow butterfly travel from the right side of the parkway to the left. Then a couple days ago, I stopped seeing it. I started wondering what happened to that butterfly.

"But then I learned that butterflies only live for three weeks. What if they only had to work, bond with family and find the one butterfly who makes their heart calm down or speed up? They wouldn't waste time on things that aren't significant, right?"

"Right."

"Close your eyes, please."

"Why?" he asked, shutting one.

"You have trust issues, Mr. Smith. I won't hurt you. Close your other eye."

The truth, spoken so gently, zinged through his chest.

"I told you a secret, and I think it's getting in the way of what could develop between us. Is that true?"

So she remembered and hadn't said a word. She'd been waiting on him. "Yes." Everything in him told him to believe her.

Alex stood and pulled him up too. She put his hands around her and slid her arms up his back. "Three weeks is a long time."

"It is a long time," he agreed.

"I want you to consider that I might be your butterfly."

He couldn't keep from smiling. "I'll consider it."

"Hunter, you're a beautiful man, and I won't compromise your ethics, but I'm going to try to get you to."

She put her face next to his and burrowed her nose in his neck. "Woman," he said, laughing, "what are you doing?"

"Giving you a reason to think about me." She gently bit his neck, kissed the bite spot and then she let him go.

The sense of loss was immediate. He opened his eyes and she was almost at the door.

"Will you pick me up in the morning or do you want to meet me at the office?"

"I'll pick you up at six-thirty," he said.

Hunter watched Alex leave. When she finally exited the parking lot, he called Chris.

"Man, I'm in trouble, and I need you to set me straight. I'm falling for Alexandria Lord Wright-Foster."

"You're what!"

"I know. Now tell me what a low-down dirty dog I am."

Chapter 10

"One million one hundred fifty-six dollars is definitely missing. If you look at these slips, they prove that Marc, not Mervyn, withdrew the money. Mr. Feinstein was correct."

Alex felt faint, the everyday china her grandmother had given her shaking in her unsteady hand.

She reached for the dinner tray she'd set up in the living room so she and Hunter could be comfortable while he reviewed the reports he'd prepared.

The plate wobbled on the wood surface, making a sickening thud when it came to its final rest. She no longer had a taste for her homemade lemon chicken picatta, even though it had taken her an hour to prepare the dish.

Sitting down next to Hunter, she gazed at the sheets of paper he'd stacked on the sectional and saw nothing but lines and numbers. He'd spent the day with her at the office and had come back to her house so they could have some privacy.

"Dinner looks good." He sampled the chicken. "It's hot. Just the way I like it."

Alex pushed Little Sweetie aside with her foot. "Go lie down, you already ate. Hunter, are you sure it's not in another account? Have you double-checked everything Mr. Feinstein sent to you?"

"I've audited all your books. A little over a million dollars."

"That can't be right. Why would Marc steal from me? I was teaching him how to loosen up and have fun. We were good for each other. He was so stuffy. Money wasn't an object for us."

Hunter nodded. "There are two ways of looking at that. But let's look at it from one per-spective. Maybe he was investing it in something for you. A vacation home."

"We shared a home on Martha's Vineyard with friends of the family. My family already owns homes in Texas and Connecticut. We only traveled abroad for our wedding. There was no need to buy another place."

"Were you looking at a cabin, maybe? Something more rural or local? A fishing cabin or something?"

"I'm not a nature kind of girl. If you're sleeping in a tent, you're not sleeping with me."

"I don't know, Alex. I'm just guessing here. You knew him better than anyone."

"Apparently not."

Hunter rubbed her leg and Alex felt the first strains of relief flow out of her that day. "Don't be too hard on yourself. There's an explanation. You just don't know what it is."

"Go ahead and eat. I'm not trying to starve you." She curled up next to him on the sofa and flipped on the flat screen. They watched a game show for a few minutes, then changed to the Turner station. An old black-and-white movie starring Audrey Hepburn played and Little Sweetie came and curled up with her.

"Hunter?"

"Hmm?" he asked, turning to the sports channel.

"Do you think he used the money to finance his relationships with Danielle and Renee?"

"No."

Alex leaned back. "How can you be so sure?"

"Because they were too worried about the insurance money. If they were independently wealthy, they wouldn't care about a couple thousand dollars."

"My policy on Marc was significantly more."

"Really? Well, that makes sense."

She got up and went to her desk to find the folder. "Why do you sound suspicious all of a sudden?"

"You're so young. Most young women don't want to talk about life insurance."

"It's one of the things you hope to never have to use, but you know, eventually somebody will."

"Yeah. By the way, this food is delicious. You made this?" he asked, looking at her legs, then her thighs. She'd changed into shorts and a T-shirt the minute she'd walked in from work. But the high heels set her outfit off.

She eased down beside him. "Yes, I know how to cook. This dish is one of my specialties."

"Do you have a million dollars to put back?"

"No."

Hunter looked as if he didn't believe her. "Your godfather seems to think so."

"He loves me, but he's delusional. I have money, but it's tied up in this condo and investments. I may have a quarter of that. But I can't bail my life out of a million-dollar problem, Hunter. Ooh." Alex squeezed her eyes shut and grit her teeth.

"What's wrong?"

"My head hurts."

"Come here. You're too young to be falling apart." On the sectional, he made her sit with her back to him and he massaged her temples. "Relax your shoulders. Put them down."

"I didn't even know they were up. Now I know why people die young. Too much stress."

"Maybe Marc thought he didn't need permission to take the money."

Alex tried not to look as frustrated as she felt. "He didn't have the right to take it. We had money, we were both working. But neither of us was spending a million dollars. We didn't have it like that. How'd he do it? One lump sum or a little at a time?"

"A little at a time."

"That tells me he knew he was being deceitful. What am I going to do?"

"Can you borrow it?"

Alex took a deep breath and let her head fall back. "Sure, but how would I pay it back? I get a small salary from the company that I just started really paying attention to. The economy is depressed right now and we've over-built. Right now I've got ten properties that aren't sold out. With no buyers, and three new properties under construction, I can't green-light new projects."

"What happens if you can't build?"

"We continue to scout new land, work our past buyers who might want to upgrade and sell the existing property in our inventory. There's always something to do."

"I'm impressed. You said you were a lightweight, but you know your stuff."

Her shoulders slid up and down slowly. "I wanted to be wildly successful. Not just marginally. I wanted to prove that I could do this job so perfectly my family wouldn't doubt me."

"But you can't now that Marc's gone."

"He didn't work with me. Marc was a great cheerleader, you know? But he stole from me. Not just money, Hunter. I was gullible. I was looking for an older man who wouldn't play silly games."

"You'd had bad experiences with guys your age?"

"I went to college for two years. All we did was party and go out. I wasted my parents' money on having a good time. I came home at twenty and decided to work."

"That's when you started at Wright Enterprises?"

"Yes. My grandfather was a stickler for my earning my paycheck. He made me get my broker's license. I'm thankful now. I know both sides of the business."

"How'd you meet Marc?"

"We met at a seminar on women improving themselves in sales. He was a presenter, and I was really into his topic *Navigating Shark-infested Waters*. He took me to dinner and wined and dined me. Treated me with respect, and I fell for him. I should have known things were too good to be true. Here I was thinking I was so clever by leaving guys my age alone when I was getting played by a master."

"You can't let that stop you from falling in love again."

"Yes, I can. I don't need love. My family is supposed to love me, and look at how they treat me. Marc was supposed to love me, and that was a mess. Had he not died, I probably would have never found out. Forget love."

Every muscle in her body ached and Alex bent over, then stretched to try to ease the pain.

"Hunter, I swear, I'm never getting married ever again."

He touched her then, caressing her arms, brushing her hair away from her face. "Don't say that. You're hurt that Marc betrayed you, and you're making generalizations."

"No, I'm not. I don't need a husband to make a living or have a baby. Go on a cruise, get old. Die."

He stroked her jaw and, despite everything, she tilted her chin toward his comforting hand. "Be quiet. You're talking nonsense."

"I am not."

"You're a hardhead. Shh," he said, and Little Sweetie yipped. "Not you, your mom. She's talking crazy."

The dog stared at them for a few seconds then lay back down. "That's the laziest dog in the world. Why are your shoulders back up?"

"You hurt my feelings."

Hunter leaned Alex back so that her hair created a pool in his lap.

"How'd I hurt your feelings?"

"You said I'm a hardhead when I'm not. I try to listen and follow everyone's directions, but everyone wants to tell me what to do, and it's hard not to yell. People think just because I'm young,

I'm not as smart as them. Now I'm being made a fool of, and you think I'm a hardhead."

"Hey," he said, stroking her cheek.

She looked at him.

"You're pouting, and I've never seen you do that before."

"It beats crying."

"Somebody told me it's good to cry," he said, caressing her hair, his gaze so tender she wanted to climb inside and languish in the comfort.

"Maybe it is. It's always been seen as a sign of weakness in my family."

"You know that's not true."

"No, I don't."

"I'm sorry, Alex."

No man had ever apologized to her. She was startled by her emotions as tears rose in her throat. She squeezed her eyes shut and the feeling dissolved, but she didn't want to tell Hunter how close he was to pushing her emotions over the edge.

Hunter kicked off his shoes. "Move over," he told her and scooted down until they were lying next to each other. Hunter threw the chenille throw she'd bought a few weeks ago over her legs. "I said I was sorry."

"I forgive you."

"I think you can do better than that," he said, and tilted her chin up and pressed his lips into hers.

Alex opened for him and licked his lips, inviting his tongue to come out and play. He kept it inside as she prodded with the tip of hers, teasing his lips in a game of seduction.

His moan signaled the wall coming down and she sealed his lips with hers, closing the deal, when their tongues met. Sparks flew. This was what she'd been missing. This body-to-body feeling of being desired.

"Don't cry, Alex," he said, kissing her cheeks. "I'm sorry."

"I'm not crying."

Tenderly he guided her lips to his jaw. "Kiss me here," he said.

She kissed his jaw and neck. "You taste good. Come on. Let's finish this work before this goes too far."

Neither moved.

Her back was to the cushions and he covered her with the blanket. She felt cocooned from the outside world. Safe from all she'd been going through. For the first time in days she didn't feel panicked or worried. Alex spread the blanket over him too and he chuckled. "I'm not cold. You're the one with shorts on."

"Why aren't you taken, Hunter? You're handsome and you're a good guy. It's hard to believe women in Atlanta leave you alone."

"I usually date older women."

Unsure what to make of his statement, she waited a few minutes. "Why?"

"In my opinion, younger women don't know what they want. An older woman knows her own mind. She's through playing games and she's formed a belief system that no one can influence. She's busy with her life and she doesn't need me to give her everything."

"Don't you want to be wanted?"

"Wanted yes, needed, no," he said.

For a moment Alex thought about what he said. "What's the difference?"

"The thing about need is that eventually it becomes a power struggle. When a person wants you, you have the option of wanting them back. When they need you, you're indentured to them. I don't want to need someone's love again."

"When did you need it before? What happened?"

He shook his head and smiled at her. "Do we have to get into this?"

"Why not? We're talking about all the dirty secrets of my life. Why not yours? Fair is fair, Hunter, the man with the trust issues."

"Fine," he said, smelling like chicken and cologne. He searched for a comfortable position, but that only worked him closer to her. Now his jeans were pressed against her midsection.

"I was with a woman named Sonia and we'd been together for a couple years. We knew each other, and I thought we'd get married once we were free from the military. She'd been in the service for four years as a medic, so she'd seen her share of injuries, and so when I got hurt, I thought we could weather the storm."

"Were you two living together?"

"Yes. We had an apartment at the base. Anyway, she got word that I was hurt, and the first thing she wanted to know was how bad. They told her, of course."

"Did she come to you? What happened?"

"She didn't come. She waited five days."

Alex looked at Hunter and it might have been the recessed lighting over the paintings, but it looked as if bars had come down across his eyes. Though years had passed, he couldn't disguise the hurt tonight. "She didn't want to be with an injured soldier. She saw the carnage daily. She didn't want to live with it. By the time she got there I was being prepped to be sent to Germany. Sonia was a very proud woman, and she explained her feelings, although I knew what was going on in her mind. We parted right then. She returned stateside, cleaned out the place and left."

"What a selfish bitch."

His laughter rippled through both of them, and his troubles escaped through the empty bubbles.

"Are you kidding me? She left you? You're a war hero. If you ask me, you got lucky. Can you imagine living with somebody that resents you for not being able to use your arm? I think your arm is very happy right now."

Hunter cradled her. His lips closed over hers, and he kissed her as gently as he could. "It is."

"Harder," she told him.

He deepened the pressure of his kiss.

"No. Hold me tighter."

"I don't want to hurt you."

"I'm not her. You can't break me."

He held her tighter and couldn't get enough of kissing her. "Tighter, Hunter."

"Baby, you're asking for trouble."

"She sure is, especially since she's still married."

Hunter nearly leaped off the sofa, but Alex held on to him.

"We do have some explaining to do."

Alex sat on her legs and noted the shocked expressions on Willa's and Jerry's faces as Hunter and Little Sweetie sat next to her. "Y'all sit down. You know Hunter. I have something serious to tell you both. I'm going to have to swear you to secrecy and then break it to the family tomorrow."

Willa took off her jacket and sat down while Jerry glowered at Hunter.

"Jerry, there's nothing to be angry about. I've got some bad news. I'm sorry to tell you but Marc died three weeks ago in a plane crash. But to complicate things even further, Marc was married to two other women."

Chapter 11

Hunter expected an explosion of questions, but Jerry and Willa embraced Alex, offering their condolences.

"Guys, I'm okay," she began, but their sadness enveloped her, wearing down her tough exterior until she had to take time to soothe their shock at her loss. Theirs, too. Marc had been Jerry's brother-in-law. He hadn't known Marc to be a cheating husband, so he had mixed emotions that vacillated between anger and disbelief.

"How could he do that to you, Alex? You're a good person," Willa consoled her.

"If he weren't dead, I'd shoot him." Jerry's words were quiet but held menace.

"Hunter, will you get us some wine? The bar is in the corner, but the ice chest isn't full." Alex's expression pleaded for patience.

"I'll take care of it."

Hunter took the ice bucket to the kitchen, got the ice and waited a few minutes, giving them some time alone. He straightened the kitchen from Alex's cooking, replaying tonight's events in his head.

There wasn't much about Alex that he didn't want, except anything long-term and she wanted to go it alone. He'd take right now, because things now would get better.

He wiped down the refrigerator not really understanding how she'd gotten seasoning on the door, but the cabinet doors over the refrigerator caught his attention. They were set back at least two feet and with Alex being so short, he'd almost bet she wouldn't put anything in them. But would Marc?

Hunter stood in front of the refrigerator and tried to reach the cabinet handles and couldn't. If Marc had wanted to hide something in plain sight, would he go for the one place Alex couldn't reach?

Excitement built in him, but he contained it.

He'd wait for Alex and they'd explore together. Too much had gone on behind her back.

Crystal wineglasses hung from the rack and he slid them down and poured the wine just as Jerry walked into the kitchen.

Hunter turned to ascertain his mood. Jerry offered his hand and they shook.

"Sorry for jumping to conclusions. My sister explained everything. I appreciate all you've done for her. She really likes you."

"I like her a lot too. I want to help her."

"She needs a lot of help."

They stood in silence, jazz serenading the quietness.

"Alex is in a bad position," Jerry went on. "My family won't stop until they get what they want from her. I'm not sure why she fights them."

He gazed through the opening at the women who hugged on the sofa. For a second, Alex rested her head on Willa's shoulder then lifted it and put her hands on Willa's cheeks. They laughed softly. Then Alex answered the phone. A moment later, she put it down and they leaned forward, talking in hushed tones.

"Alex believes in Wright Enterprises. She told me how your grandfather made her get her broker's license. She's got the skills, but no respect. You could help her by being her biggest supporter."

"I am, but I don't want any part of the company."

Surprised, Hunter looked at him. "Does she know?"

"No, but I'll tell her in good time. Look at them. That's the way I like to see them. Young and happy."

"She's a grown-up, too, Jerry. She can handle being an adult. Give her some credit. She knows what she's doing. She *wants* the responsibility."

"You sure?" he said, still looking at his sister through rose-colored glasses.

"Positive. Keep an eye on her and see for yourself."

Hunter thought about the letter Alex had received a few days ago. The handwriting looked feminine, but that was to his untrained eye. It could have been male. He could have been trying to warn her to leave while she still had a shot at being happy. Hunter hoped Jerry would stay loyal to Alex. She needed a soldier in her corner.

"You want to grab that for Willa?"

"Sure." Jerry picked up the glass. "You're going

to help her get to the bottom of this mess about Marc? About whether she's his real wife or not?"

"Yes."

"And then?"

"Whatever else she needs. We're together in this," Hunter told him.

"I got that when we walked in. Are you worried at all that it's a rebound relationship?"

"No. Alex and Marc had a lot going on. I'm not trying to take his place. We've got something different. All I can say is that I've never done this before and neither has she. So we're in this new territory together."

"I've been there. You've got to live for today. I'm there with Willa."

"She's cute," Hunter said, watching the girls blot each others tears. "I think they might need another minute."

"Yeah, they cry about anything," Jerry said with a shake of his head.

The men shook their heads, confused.

"You hungry? We've got some extra chicken," Hunter offered, not wanting to walk back in the living room yet.

"Sure," Jerry said. "Why not."

Hunter opened cabinets and pulled down more

plates and served up the food. He looked back at the cabinet over the refrigerator, believing in his heart it held some of Marc's secrets.

"You won't desert her?" Jerry asked.

"No. Never." He'd never said that before and his injured heart skipped a beat. He would definitely go home tonight to regroup.

"Good. She doesn't deserve that."

"I'm not that kind of man. But can you do me a favor?

"When you get in those meetings with your father and brother, stand up for her. She needs support. She worries that no one is there to help her."

"I didn't realize how important that was to her. I thought she had them under control. They're pissed as hell that she keeps having Mervyn thrown in jail. He's scared of her now."

"No kidding." Hunter laughed and Jerry joined him.

"Yeah, and *dad* doesn't know what to do. Alex actually has him worried that he won't have the company he grew up in to run in his old age. She's making them accountable and he's scared. I wish they could meet halfway, but he hasn't been nice to her and she isn't budging on how things should be run."

"Good. She'll be glad to hear that. Will you ask Willa to send an e-mail requesting your dad and brother be at the meeting at ten? That should give Alex enough time to get in and get her thoughts together about how she's going to tell them about Marc."

"No problem." Jerry peered at the girls again. "Willa's the sweetest woman I've ever met. I hope she'll marry me one day."

"You got it bad for her, don't you?"

"I played professional football for five years and had I don't know how many concussions. That last one almost killed me. I was in a coma for five days. I've looked death in the eye, and now I know what's important. The company isn't it. My sister needs to focus on her personal life and be happy. She doesn't understand that nothing inside the doors of Wright Enterprises will bring her happiness. When I walked in here tonight I was pissed off. But hearing what I've heard, I know what she needs to do. Move on."

"Did you talk much to Marc?"

"Sure, but not about anything in particular. He was a likable guy. He blended well. That was the thing with him. He traveled a lot, knew a lot about a lot of things, and he seemed to love Alex. That was important to me. She seemed happy. He liked to cook. He was always in the spices, always in the cabinets looking for something or another. Ordering things from places nobody had ever heard of. I'm a bachelor. I came a lot of times just to eat. Damn liar." Jerry pulled silverware from the drawer and carried the wine into the living room to the ladies.

Hunter stacked the last dish in the dishwasher and waited for Alex to finish her goodbyes at the door. He heard it close just as he pressed the button to start the machine and wiped down the stove and sink. Everything else was clean. He leaned against the counter as she appeared in the doorway, her heels clicking against the hardwood in soft taps, Little Sweetie asleep in her arms.

Even after fifteen hours, Alex still looked sexy. Hunter knew it was time for him to go home. He could only get in trouble from here. "Mr. Smith?"

"Ma'am?"

"My brother is sleeping with my assistant."

He chuckled. "I figured as much after our talk tonight."

"They left because they thought we wanted to be alone."

"Where would they get that idea?"

"Could be because I was kissing you when they walked in," she said, standing in front of him.

"You were kissing me? I thought I was kissing you?"

"My memory is foggy. I might need an instant replay."

She put Little Sweetie in his doggie bed by the deck door and tiptoed back to Hunter with her arms outstretched. She wasn't smiling, and even though he knew kissing her now was a bad idea, stopping wasn't an option.

He caught her, lifting her off her feet.

She didn't kiss him as he expected. She held him for a long time and when he tried to let her go she wouldn't release him. "What's wrong?"

"Renee and Danielle called while you were in the kitchen with Jerry. The attorney wants to meet with us day after tomorrow at two o'clock. They have reached a decision."

Her heart pounded and he held her tighter. "Yes, that's it," she whispered. "Tighter."

"Come on." Hunter tabled the idea about looking in the cabinet tonight. Whatever might be there would keep.

"You're staying," she said as he walked her down the wide hallway to her bedroom.

"Unless you plan on kicking me out."

"No, baby. You're staying."

Chapter 12

Hunter pulled his clothes off and sat at the foot of Alex's bed, bringing her between his legs. He kissed her and noticed that she was more subdued.

"What's the matter?" he asked, kissing her knuckles and the palm of her hand.

"I need to shower. I'll be back in five minutes."

She had the hem of her T-shirt in her hands and he lifted it enough to kiss her stomach.

"Four minutes," she whispered, slipping out of one heel, limping on the other one. "I promise I'll smell nice and sweet." She pulled the T-shirt over her head and let it hit the floor.

He brought her closer, tasting her lips and neck, getting lost in the soft sensuality of her hair. "I like you just like this." He pushed her shorts down the backs of her thighs, enjoying the feel of her skin against his hands. With his knees he kept her legs open so he could touch her smoothly shaved secrets. He ran his lips along her collarbone, wanting to make her breath come faster, make her head fall back, his name to drip from her lips until dawn splashed in orange and blues across the sky.

"Marc always liked for me to shower—"

He looked into her cinnamon-colored eyes and he kissed her hard until her mouth hung open. "This is you and me."

"I didn't mean that." For a second she looked as if she'd committed an unforgivable sin, then he wrapped his arms around her and sucked her breasts until her moans nearly made him lose control.

He nudged her shorts all the way down, then pulled her to him by her bottom and squeezed until she brought her arms up and around his neck. "How does that feel?" he asked, running his mouth down her neck.

"Good."

He squeezed her butt until she was up on her toes. "How does that feel?"

"It hurts."

"Then you tell me what hurts." His hands gentled and he kissed her, long and slow.

He unhooked her bra and her breasts slipped from the satin. They were already wet from his attention, but he liked that he was free to enjoy them at will.

"Yes," she whispered, her hands against his cheeks.

"I didn't hear you, baby." He continued the ministrations, alternating between hard and soft, amazed that her nipples grew an inch in size on his tongue.

"Yes, that feels good. This one too."

Suddenly Hunter pulled the bedspread off the bed and threw it on the floor, pulling Alex down with him. Caught off guard, she started laughing. "You're crazy. What are you doing?"

"Making love to you. You're a sexy, desirable woman, and you're acting like you've never done this before."

He sucked her breasts hard until she pushed at his head and forced him to kiss her mouth. Their tongues tangled in a battle that ended with her biting his jaw, her teeth gliding down his chin to his neck.

"Yeah, baby."

"That felt so good it hurt," she told him, laughing. "You knew it."

He kissed her breasts softly, making up. "I know. Tell me what you want. Tell me what feels good. Make some noise, girl. You're a part of this."

"Okay," she whispered.

"You're doing that again?" Before she knew what was going on, he flipped her over and bit her left cheek.

"Okay!" she said loudly, twisting when he bit her butt again.

"You want a cat, you got a cat."

Flipping him, she rolled on top of Hunter and wrestled with him, their mouths mating in a battle of tongues and teeth. She tasted him with her whole mouth, letting her taste buds absorb the flavor of him as she slid her lips down over his entire body.

His fingers stretched her out and pulled at her, cupped her and caressed her, brought her to climax again and again, and made her cry out until she was hoarse.

When they were ready, she rolled a condom down him, and he entered her from behind as she lay on her side, as he whispered sweet words of ecstasy in her ear.

Alex felt her most powerful climax building, and told him.

"After you, baby," he said.

And he meant it.

Alex opened one eye as she felt herself being lifted. She knew it was Hunter, but didn't know where he was taking her.

Hunter laid her on the bed and sat beside her, his chest still bare. He had so many scars she wanted to ask him about, but more than that she wanted him to stay with her.

"What more can you do to me?" she teased, her voice sleepy, her body completely relaxed.

"That's not the endorsement I was hoping for. Maybe we should start all over."

"Yes, tomorrow."

He covered her with the blanket. "You need your rest and I need to go home."

"You can't leave. It's too late."

"And I can't show up to work in the same clothes. I'll be back at six-thirty."

She didn't know when he'd lit the built-in fireplace, but it flamed in orange licks over the gas logs. Making love had never before left her so completely satiated.

So this is what everyone had been talking about. Alex was more than comfortable. This was the perfect fantasy. Why couldn't this feeling last forever?

Because fantasies weren't real.

Tomorrow's hell was just a few hours away and her life was going to continue to change.

He pulled on his shirt and she felt a tiny measure of disappointment that all the pleasure he'd coaxed from her was leaving with him. "Are you going to be all right? Want me to come with you?" she asked.

He chuckled. "Alex, I'm a guy."

"I'll protect you, Hunter."

He twisted on the bed and for a long time he stared into her eyes. She waited, wanting him to express himself.

He smoothed her hair over her breast.

"Girl, you're something else. But thank you. I'm coming up early in the morning. Be ready."

"Okay."

Hunter buried his face in her hair and gave her a sloppy wet kiss that left her giggling until she fell asleep.

Chapter 13

"You left here knowing that your husband was dead and you didn't tell us? What were you trying to hide?"

The entire Wright family had come for the emergency meeting and Alex was the star of the show. Dressed conservatively in a cream-colored suit, gray pearls, her hair pulled back in a bun, she looked the part but seemed ready for the worst.

The meeting hadn't been going for more than five minutes and her father had already started yelling. Mervyn Jr. and Jerry were seated across from each other, but neither had spoken to the other.

Mervyn Sr. hadn't even offered condolences.

Hunter couldn't stand the man.

He'd walked in with a bad attitude, slamming a folder on the table as if he was establishing his authority right then. To Alex's credit she didn't blink, but continued with her instructions to Willa.

Refreshments were brought into the room and Hunter poured himself and Alex a cup of tea.

The cup rattled against the saucer each time he jarred the table. And each time the cup rattled, Alex jumped ever so slightly.

Mervyn Sr. seemed ready to eat her alive. He marched around the table, gesturing wildly, moving behind Alex's chair, shouting, and she flinched one too many times.

"You act like you can just come in and dictate how things are run around here, and you can't. I don't take orders from you, Alexandria. You may have controlling interest in the company, but you will not tell me what to do!"

Hunter got up. "Take your seat and conduct yourself like a professional, or you're excused."

Incredulous, Mervyn Sr. looked at his daughter. "You've got a henchman, now? You replaced your husband with a bodyguard?"

Alex folded her hands on the table. "Dad, we're waiting on you. Please, have a seat."

"This is an outrage," he said, but sat down next to Mervyn Jr. who hadn't said a word.

"To answer your first question, I wasn't trying to hide anything," Alex began. "I left here believing Marc was alive. I went to find out for sure. I was wrong. I'm sorry to have kept it quiet for so long, but I've had a lot to deal with."

"What else? We're your family, Alexandria. What else are you hiding?"

"Marc had other business that will take me away from time to time until it's all settled. So we'll need to pull together and work as a family. I'm prepared to offer you your job back, Mervyn, if you'd like to come back."

Her brother glowered at her and grunted, looked at the table and didn't respond.

"Well, good luck then. Right now the economy is in a recession. We've got to watch our money carefully. Instructions were left—"

"Your husband hasn't been dead a month and you have a new boyfriend?" her father practically screamed. Hunter wished he could give the old man a real reason to scream, but this was Alex's family.

How she'd dealt with them all her life was beyond him.

"My personal relationship with Hunter is none of your business, Dad. But just so you know, Hunter is important to me. Let me tell you something else…if I ever come back and find that one thing has been changed in the company without my consent, you won't have a job either. You're disrespectful and mean. Grandma Letty would have never tolerated this. She gave me controlling interest in this company for a reason. Hasn't anyone ever wondered why?"

"I have."

Alex rushed to her feet. "Mother."

The entire family stood and Mervyn Sr. ran over to help his wife. "Thank you, Mervyn. It's good to see you."

Hunter watched the entire family snap to attention as the most beautiful woman he'd ever seen walked into the room.

Alex's mother had long wavy silver and gray hair that hung past her shoulders, with flawless skin the color of sand. She moved with a slow grace, leaning heavily on a black cane with a gold handle.

No one spoke as she entered and walked toward the table, but they were all surprised to see her. Alex had told him she was a virtual recluse.

"Dorothy," Mervyn Sr. said, "I'll be home in a few hours. We can talk then."

"How old are you, Alexandria?"

"Twenty-three, Mama."

"We haven't talked in twenty-three years, Mervyn. Why would we start now?"

Hunter winked at Alex and she jutted her left hip out at him, then composed herself and watched her mother.

"Mervyn, take me up to sit next to my baby."

"No. You can sit next to me."

"I can sleep next to you, too, but I don't. Do I?"

"No, Dorothy," he said, his head down like his son's.

"And I didn't decide that, you did. A long time ago. Now, what did I say?"

Everyone held their breath while Dorothy Wright was seated at the conference table next to her daughter.

The balance of power had shifted.

Dorothy leaned her cane against the table.

"I apologize for being late. Alexandria had an announcement and nobody thought I was important enough to come to the family meeting except my daughter, who offered me car service. She's been offering me rides to these meeting every month for three years. I always said no. Today I said yes. What was your announcement, Alexandria?"

"Mama, Marc died in a plane crash three weeks ago."

Mrs. Wright's head went down for a moment then she whispered amen. "I'm so sorry for your loss. My baby's a bride and a widow. You holding up okay?"

"Yes, ma'am. I've got so much to tell you, Mama."

Hunter's heart twisted and he wished it wasn't involved with his feelings for Alex.

"Okay." Her mother studied her for a long moment, then looked at Hunter. He felt as if he'd met a disciple. "I'm Dorothy. Come talk to me sometime."

Hunter shook her hand. "Pleased to meet you. Hunter Smith."

Dorothy smiled at him. "Yes, sir. I like you very much. Now, I've got something to say."

Hunter went and stood behind Alex. He did the one thing he said he wouldn't and caressed her arm. Mervyn Jr. saw him and shot him a dirty look.

"Go ahead, Mama. You have the floor," Alex said.

"It seems to me that there's a lot of funny business going on in this family. Members are fighting against member. Folks are stealing from the family. People are doing things they know are wrong to each other in the name of money. So this is what I'm going to do. I own fourteen percent of the company stock, and I was going to give it to my grandchildren."

Mervyn Jr. slapped the table. "That's right, Mama! Give them to me. With mine and yours combined with Daddy's, I have the majority. I'll show you, Alex! I know what I'm doing. I'll show you how to run this company from the outside. You're out and I'm in. Thank you, Mama. Thank you."

He laughed, his eyes watery, the strain he'd been under showing in his cracked features. He wiped his nose. "She's giving them to me. Right?" he said to his father. "That's right. Right?"

A heavy silence stretched into an even longer minute.

Hunter tried not to think about shooting Alex's

brother. He looked like a junkie and probably was but had been able to disguise it with all the money he'd been taking.

"Daddy, we should be celebrating," Mervyn Jr. told him.

"Shut up," his father said under his breath.

"Okay, Mama." Alex sat tall in her chair. "If that's your decision, I respect it. I'm so glad you came down here to see us." She grasped her mother's hand. "And I'm glad you go out of the house. You're so brave. I love you."

"Hold on a minute. I said I *was going* to give them to the kids. But I'm not." She looked at her oldest son.

"Mervyn Jr., when you were stealing that money all these years, you were stealing from all of us. That's like coming into mom and your daddy's house and walking off with some of our furniture. Or walking off with your grandma's jewelry, or your granddaddy's war medals. I can't reward you for that. Your outburst just now proves you're not thinking about us, only yourself. That's the same reason I can't give the stock to my husband. I listened to how you treated this girl, and you're so disrespectful, it's sad. No. My shares go to Jerry.

'Cause he and Alex will do the right thing for this company."

She reached inside her purse and passed an envelope to her youngest son. He smiled at his mother and then came around and hugged her.

"Mama, I gotta tell you, I don't want any part of this," Jerry said. "Alex knows she can count on me to answer the phones, but I've got a less complicated lifestyle in mind, and it's about being happy with Willa. So I'm bowing out. Alex gets my shares."

"You see what I mean? I knew you'd do the right thing," their mother said.

Mervyn Jr. started crying and Mervyn Sr. leaped to his feet. "Fine. I quit. But I'm taking my biggest clients with me."

"You're not quitting, Mervyn," Dorothy told him. "Our health insurance is here and we need that. The company you spent a good part of your life in is here. You're going to get your pride off the floor and drive it and me home. Then you and I are going to have a talk. You're going to come back tomorrow and work with our daughter to continue this company's success.

"There's more going on with the money in this company. It needs to get resolved and quickly."

"Mama, what are you talking about?" Mervyn Jr. demanded.

"This meeting is adjourned," Alex declared.

"We're owed some kind of explanation, because if there's more money missing, we need to know all about it. You ruined my life. I want the same treatment for anyone else."

Alex nearly stumbled over the chair as she tried to get around it. "Mervyn, you're being irrational. You're too stubborn to take your job back, so fine. You won't get a second chance. But you're not dictating what goes on here."

"I ought to—" he said with a menacing twist to his lip.

"Son," his father said, trying to keep his voice under control. "I already told you to shut up. I'm taking your mother home. Where are you going?"

Mervyn Jr. looked at all of his family, but he saved his most scathing glare for Alex. "You're going to get what you deserve."

"You're not going to touch a hair on her head. But I welcome your effort," Hunter said and stepped in front of Alex.

Mervyn Jr. slammed out the door and walked away. Everyone watched his stormy exit but said nothing.

"Daddy, Mama?" Alexandria said. "He's not allowed back in the building. He scares the employees, and I don't feel safe when he's here."

"Mervyn hasn't ever hurt anyone. There's never been any proof of that," their father said.

"I'm not going to let him hurt anyone," Jerry said. "He's ridiculous. I loaned him some money last week to pay his bills, but his ex, Danisha, called and said he didn't pay them and the water was disconnected."

"How are she and the kid making it?" Alex asked, and Hunter could see the guilt she was shouldering. She wasn't hard enough to be a corporate raider. She was still very young and easily influenced. Her family was manipulating her and she didn't recognize it.

"Danisha has a job so she paid the bill," Jerry told them. "But she was just expecting the money from Mervyn."

"From my experience, he looks like he may be on drugs," Hunter added. "It's best if you all take extra precautions. He threatened Alex twice and all of you were here. What if you hadn't been able to stop him? You say he's never done this before, but he did it and in front of his mother and father. Think about this, what won't he do?"

Mervyn Sr. waved his hand in the air. "Fine. I'll deal with him."

Dorothy shook her head. "If he's on drugs, that's only going to land him in bigger trouble. Mervyn, take me home. I'm tired and then you need to look after the monster you created before he hurts someone or gets hurt."

Mervyn Sr. looked around at the unsympathetic eyes of his family. "I'll get the car. Jerry, bring Mother to the lobby."

"Dad—" Alex said.

He looked at Alex and walked out.

"Wow. Well," she said, then didn't say anything else.

"Corporate America is a terrible place," Dorothy predicted. "Make sure you want to be here. I'll expect to see you two very soon when the three of us can get better acquainted."

Alex bent down in front of her mother. "Thank you for coming. I know this was at a great sacrifice to you."

"It's not so bad once I'm out, but it's leaving the house that shakes me up."

"Thank you. I love you." Alex kissed her mother's cheek.

"Mama, this chair is on wheels. How about I take you for a drive," Jerry offered.

Her eyes lit up and Hunter smiled. "Now, I'm not one of those football guys you can run into things. You take it slow and we'll see how I like it."

Jerry spun the chair around one time for fun and Hunter held the door. "Hold your feet up, Dorothy. You'll have fun."

"I'm taking your word for it."

Jerry pushed her, and Dorothy's face lit up like she'd won some money. Once they got into the lobby Hunter headed back to the conference room and Alex. He thought she'd be crying or near a breakdown.

But she was wrestling with her jacket.

"You're like a kid that can't wait to get out of her church clothes. Don't you have an office where you can strip in private?"

"No. I've never had an office. I always sat at the front desk with Willa."

The jacket flew out of the tiny kitchen to the chair. The hairpins were next hitting the bottom of the waste can.

"You're kidding. You haven't had an office ever since you came back from California?"

"Yes, I like it out there, but now I have too much stuff. So, I was thinking of moving into my grandmother's office. The auditors were in there and now they're gone. And now I've got you to think about."

Hunter walked into the kitchenette to find her wrestling her sleeveless sweater over her head.

He kissed under her arm and took a love bite out of her triceps.

She squealed. "That tickles."

"You look like you're okay," he said.

"I am. I hate that my brother blames me for his troubles, but that's what people do when they don't want to take responsibility. I've got two very big items on my agenda for the day. One going home. Two making sure I get there within a half hour because my new bed is being delivered."

"Your new what?"

"Bed. Can you help me?" she said, leaving the tiny bathroom and meeting him in the kitchenette. "Put your hands there."

She stood in front of him in a black bra, cream skirt and cream shoes, her hair cascading over her shoulder.

"Squeeze my tush right there." He looked behind her and followed her request.

She leaned back and fluffed out her curls, her eyes half closed, the gold hoop earrings flat against a blanket of dark hair.

When she leaned up she put her arms around his neck.

"What's this called again?" he asked, squeezing her bottom again.

"It's a tush." She kissed his neck above the open collar of his shirt. "Harder, please."

She caressed the back of his head and gave him a love bite on the neck.

"Girl, where are you going with this?"

"Squeeze a little…" She sucked in a deep breath. "Oh, that's good. Now hold me right there."

"Good for whom? I'm suffering, and I can't leave the building like this. I know I can't walk. So who's benefiting?"

"Oh, I am and you are too. You ended my drought. Now I can't get enough. Let's go back to my place."

"No. One of the rules was no fooling around during the hours of nine to five."

"But this is a celebration."

"It's still daytime," he told her, his thumb riding over her butt. He couldn't stop remembering how good it was to be with a totally uninhibited woman. Once she got over her insecurity, their lovemaking had taken on a new dimension.

"But it's my lunch hour and I need to go home, Hunter. So let's go home and we'll come back after lunch."

"No fooling around."

"If you say so." She was still pressed against him. "You've got to make the first move."

He released her and she walked off, pulling her jacket on over her bra and fastening it. There was nothing between her neck and cleavage but pearls.

"What about your top?" he asked.

"I think you need it more than me," she said and left the conference room with her papers and leather briefcase.

Hunter followed, her shirt shielding his uncomfortable hard-on.

Chapter 14

Hunter wished he were driving Alex down the Pacific Coast Highway. Instead, they were making their way through the side streets of Decatur.

If he had to face the same level of hostility that Alex did every day at work, he wouldn't own his company, or those people wouldn't work for him. As the hot sun beat down on his skin, it cleansed his bad mood, and it felt good to have Alex beside him with her hair flowing in the wind and her hand resting on the back of his seat.

She suddenly dug in her bag and pulled out a card from Willa. She read aloud, "'Your bed's all set up and the other one donated. Little Sweetie is with me for a couple days, if you don't mind. My new puppy can't stand being alone. Love, Willa.'"

Alex adjusted in her seat and turned toward him a little. "I have the most efficient assistant in the world.

"She's good and she likes you. I like her too," she said, digging for more papers, pulling out another folder.

"What you got there?"

"Papers from the audit."

Quietly she studied them and wrote questions at the top of each page and he wished he had her in her new bed, tossing all those papers in her fireplace. Her family was crazy, with the exception of Jerry and her mother. The only reason she questioned her mental acumen was because her father and brother had god complexes. They were ridiculous.

The emotional abuse they'd inflicted on the family had been pervasive for too long. Alex needed to be away from them. Now he understood her reason for marrying Marc.

He legitimized her to her family. He was an older man who was a solid citizen with a steady job. If they knew he was a polygamist and a thief, she'd never hear the end of it. As far as Hunter was concerned, they needed to know that information.

"Is it possible that Marc simply blew the money or gambled it away?" she asked.

"It is, but I didn't see a single shred of evidence that he gambled. Let me ask you something. What's in the cabinet over the refrigerator?"

"Nothing. I can't reach it. I don't know why the builders put the cabinets up that high."

"Jerry said Marc did most of the cooking."

"I did my share, but Marc worked from home. This bank statement that you gave me says he took fifty thousand dollars out of the account a week before he died. What happened to that money?"

Hunter stopped at the light. "I don't know, but it might explain why he was in Philadelphia, and why he went to California."

"Chris never did explain that," Alex said. "Why'd you ask me about the cabinet?"

"You said he never kept any papers at home, but he had to have kept papers somewhere. He was always cooking. I thought maybe he stashed something in the kitchen."

Alex pushed her hair back, thinking. "I don't know. I've never given that cabinet a second thought."

"I think he did keep things hidden, but you ladies just didn't know it. I believe he hid things in plain sight. That's the way people like him think. He didn't travel on commercial airlines. Didn't stay in hotels. Changed jobs every couple years, worked out of his home. Cell phones. He was slick to have three wives and not leave a paper trail. You have a few clothes and a few pictures of him, but nothing else."

"Right. No family members. I believed he was an orphan. He told me he traveled a lot. Right from the beginning. If I couldn't handle it, I couldn't be with him."

"He was laying the groundwork."

"Well, he already had two wives. He knew what would work." Alex rubbed her forehead. "What I don't get is why I didn't suspect something. I don't let people into my world. I have friends. I didn't need him."

"He was a master manipulator. People like him make mistakes. We're going to find his mistakes and we're going to fix them."

Alex gave him a sidelong look. "You think something might be in that cabinet?"

"It's worth a look."

"We'll find out. What happens then?"

"Depends on what we find. If it's money, you put it back. If it's paperwork, we go through it with a fine-tooth comb and decide how we're going to approach it. Marc had secrets. Our job is to uncover them and do what's right for you."

"What about Renee and Danielle?" Alex asked. "What if he's stolen from them?"

"We'll find out tomorrow at the meeting. I doubt that he left paperwork of theirs in your home. That's too risky. If you found it, he'd have too much explaining to do."

"Yeah, he lied about having a brother. I doubt that he'd admit to having two other wives."

The sun burned full force as Alex searched for her sunglasses. Sliding them in place, she leaned back and stretched her arm out the passenger window. "I think I'll buy a convertible."

Hunter got an eyeful. "A sexy car for a sexy woman."

"Maybe next year when everything settles down. I never knew a man could be such a liar. Not a man that I was involved with. Men are such liars."

"Hey, don't paint all men with the same brush, Alex. You know good men."

"Who? You saw my shining examples today. Except for you and Jerry, I'm not doing so well."

"Fifty percent is better than zero."

"You're right."

Hunter pulled into the parking garage and backed into the space next to Alex's BMW. He studied the garage for a moment before starting the car again. "We're leaving."

"Why?" Alex sat up, looking around.

He put his hand on her midsection and made her lean back.

"Mervyn and another man are in that black four-door sedan six cars to the right. Recognize it?"

"No."

"Does he know anyone else in the building?"

"Not that I know of."

"My guess is he's waiting for you."

"Why?"

The driver got out of the car.

"I'm taking you to the front of the building. You stay with the doorman and let me handle this."

"No. That's my brother."

"What did you hire me for?" he said forcefully and she jumped.

Alex closed her eyes and then squeezed them.

"My way, Alex," he told her.

She nodded.

He left the lot and pulled in front of the building. Opening her door, he left her with the doorman. "Scottie, don't let her out of your sight."

"Trouble, Hunter?"

Alex looked between them. "You know him?"

"Scottie will explain." Hunter gave the man a card. "Call and tell Samia to run this tag. It had Jersey plates. There was one on the front."

Scottie wrote down the tag Hunter told him and then escorted Alex inside.

She waited, speculating as to what was going on but coming up with nothing good.

Alex worried over Hunter. Mervyn was there for money. There was no other reason. He probably wanted his job back too, but that wasn't going to happen.

He'd threatened her earlier and that wasn't going to go away with a quick "I'm sorry."

Pacing, Alex continued to worry about Hunter. She reached for her cell phone but it was in the car.

"Don't you have security cameras in the parking lot," she said to Scottie, looking at his simple workstation, which consisted of little more than a podium and a phone.

"Not up here we don't."

"I thought that's what part of the four-hundred-dollar-a-month condo association fee was for."

"You'll have to ask management, Mrs. Wright-Foster. I know they're installing a new one, but I don't know the details. I'm sorry."

"Thanks. I'll do that." Alex rubbed the back of her neck and counted to a hundred, and Hunter came around the corner and she rushed outside.

"Where is Mervyn?" she asked, looking past him.

"Let's talk about it upstairs."

"Everything okay?" Scottie asked, looking concerned.

"It's good. Did you reach Samia?"

"She said for you to call her when you get in."

Hunter folded a bill into Scottie's hand. "Good man. Thanks."

"Anytime, Hunter."

Hunter guided Alex into the elevator.

They walked inside her condo and she turned on him. "What's wrong?"

"Come in the living room and sit down. You know, your brother has serious problems." Hunter grasped her hands. "He came here to rob you."

"Me?" Alex put her hand to her throat. "Mervyn?"

"Yes, and he brought a friend to take care of me."

She was on her feet. "Okay, you know what? I've heard enough. We're leaving."

"Where are we going?"

"To a hotel that has security."

"What hotel is that?"

"I don't know, but if I'm not safe here, then what should I do? Let him hurt me? Let another man take advantage of me? Bring you into my life and let you get hurt? I can't have that."

Hunter brought her back to the couch. "Sweetheart, I'm the security agent." He took all the things she gathered out of her hands and sat her down. "We're going to go on with our plans."

"And those are?"

"The kitchen cabinet."

Alex folded her lips into her mouth and shook her head. "Wait just a minute. My brother came here to rob me. What does he think I have?"

"Jewelry, money. It doesn't matter. He's taken care of."

"What happened down there?"

"I called a friend, and Mervyn is on his way to a hospital where he won't be getting out for at least three days. Longer if he knows what's best for him."

"What's that mean? A mental institution?"

"A rehabilitation center. I made the call right from the lot and Mervyn was picked up and is on his way to the facility now. But Mervyn knows something's going on with the money, so the sooner we get this settled the better."

"Understood. What about his friend?"

"At the sound of the word *cop*, he took off. I don't think he'll be back."

"You did all that in that short period of time?"

"I never work alone, and I never work with only one plan."

Alex had been listening to him with the heel of her right hand on her temple. She reached out and grasped his hand, pulling him to her.

She put her head against his neck, and his whole body accepted her. "Thank you so much. I swear I don't know where I'd be without you."

He thought about giving her new bed a test run, but then remembered he was on the job. "Hey? Come on. Let's figure out the rest of this mystery."

She looked up at him through hooded eyes.

"Okay. Let's take a look."

Hunter grabbed a dining-room chair and put it against the refrigerator. He offered her a hand up.

"No, you go up and hand me anything that's up there."

He climbed up on the chair and looked down. "Catch me if I fall."

Alex smiled. "Of course, dear."

Hunter opened the cabinet doors.

"See anything?" she asked.

"Nothing was supposed to be in here, correct?"

"Correct."

"Then we've hit the mother lode."

Chapter 15

Sipping white wine, Alex flipped open one of the folders Hunter had found in the cabinet. "I knew I'd seen him with these. I'm not crazy." She pressed the seam flat with her French-manicured finger. A faraway look stole her focus.

"They're contracts for a boat. Did you know he was buying a boat?" Hunter asked, admiring the vessel.

"That's no boat," she corrected him gently. "That's a yacht. A couple girlfriends and I were invited to the launch of this line a couple years ago."

"You and a couple girlfriends? I'll bet it was a helluva party," he said, watching her.

"I was single and didn't mind being arm candy." She pursed her lips, studying the brochure and then the contract. "Maybe Marc was in California to complete the transaction. What's the sale date?"

Hunter verified what he'd just read. "Last month. But Atlanta's closer to the coast of Florida. So why take possession of it in California if he's not planning to keep it down there?"

"We're speculating as to why he was in California. We don't know for sure. What else is in the folders?"

"A receipt for interior remodeling of the boat," Hunter said. "Says final on the bottom."

"How much was that?"

"Fifty thousand dollars. Here's an address. The boat's here in Georgia. Do you have Marc's keys?"

Alex looked around. "No. The only keys I saw were the ones Renee said were hers. But if the folders were in the cabinet, the key must be here somewhere."

"I just remembered something. Where are the bank statements?"

"On the dining-room table."

They headed to the table where everything was divided by month. Hunter flipped through the statements then plucked up a page. "He withdrew fifty thousand dollars last month to pay off the boat. See here?"

Alex leaned in. "Yes. It's just more proof."

"Let's see if there's a key."

Hunter went back to the cabinet and climbed up. "There's no key ring."

"No single key?" she asked, her face turned up earnestly.

He felt around in the corners of the cabinet and hit an object. "Well, well, Ms. Alex. What do have we here?" Looking down, he smiled at her, waving two keys.

"Why, one of them must be an object that can make a luxury yacht go really fast with your wife's stolen money. I don't know about the other key, though."

"Maybe to that address," he said, pointing to the paper in her hand. "You have the title. You can sell the boat and recoup your money."

"I don't know anything about selling yachts. I guess I can look on the Internet. I can ask Jerry." She sounded defeated and tired. As if she didn't want to do another thing. She pulled

her hair on top of her head and closed her eyes
in disgust.

"Hey."

Her eyes washed him in warmth as the sun had
no more than an hour ago. Again, he wanted to
be riding down the coast with her. "I'll help you."
He wanted to add "forever," but that word wasn't
part of his vocabulary.

Walking back to the living room, they sat next
to one another on the sofa.

"Thank you," she said softly. She put her chin
on his shoulder. "I wanted to ask you, but you've
done so much already."

"Come on. Don't get shy now." He shook her
knee. "Marc made these purchases with joint
assets, but they're in his name only. If you're not
his legal wife, you might have to turn over the
assets to whomever that individual is."

Rising, Alex walked to the windows overlooking the square.

"Renee mentioned that. I'll add my name to
the documents, and if it comes to a legal battle,
they'll have to prove it's not my money he bought
them with, and not my property. My godfather
was right in that regard. I have the resources to
fight, and I will."

One thing Hunter understood was power. Alexandria now understood wealth and power.

"You up for a field trip?" he asked.

"Where?"

"I was thinking you might like to go find your new yacht."

"I thought we were waiting until tomorrow?"

"While you're still Mrs. Marc Foster, you should get the title changed on the paperwork. You've got the death certificate, right?"

"Yes." Dawning brightened her eyes. "Yes. That's a great idea."

"Where you going?" he asked as he headed for the front door and she headed toward her room.

"I have to change. I can't wear this to go yacht hunting."

"Bring some clothes for tomorrow and your toiletries," he called after her.

Already in her room, Alex stuck her head around the corner. "Why?"

Hunter waited down the hall. "Afterward you're coming home with me."

A slow smile crept over her. "All right. I'll be five minutes."

"I'm getting something to drink. Want anything?"

"No. Help yourself."

Hunter walked into the kitchen and got up on the chair. There lay a document flat on the surface that he hadn't pulled out, having left it intentionally.

He read it, hating a man he'd never known. He folded the paper, making the edges meet evenly, before slipping it into his pants pocket.

Alex would never see it. She would never know that Marc had been planning to divorce her.

Hunter drove through Atlanta heading north on I-75. He and Alex settled on letting the radio entertain them the whole way.

He questioned her about her mother's agoraphobia and the depression that kept her cooped up in the house, and she got him to open up and talk about the lonely years after his parents died in his early twenties.

The hour-and-a-half ride passed quickly before it ended near Lake Allatoona, and they turned onto the Mason Boat Storage property.

Hunter and Alex went inside the office, showed the paperwork, and were given the electronic code to use after they unlocked the door with the key.

Each metal door resembled a garage unit, but

was triple the size of a residential garage door. They parked in front of their door as instructed.

Hunter got out and opened Alex's door. "You ready?"

"As I'll ever be." Alex sounded quietly confident. He guessed she was incapable of surprise now where Marc was concerned. "Do you know how this is done?" she asked.

"We unlock the door with the key, sweetheart. Put the code in and then it goes up."

She could tell he was joking, and cut her eyes at him.

"Let's give it a try," she said. Alex slipped her hand in his. "I'm ready."

"You got the key?" he asked.

"I sure do." Alex inserted the key, twisted, and the chamber released. "This is for real."

Hunter tapped in the code and the door started up.

For some reason they both took one giant step back as the magnificent yacht came into view. "Wow. I've got to hand it to him. My husband had great taste."

"In more ways than one," Hunter said. She squeezed his hand a little tighter, but kept her gaze on the yacht.

"What about the car?" she asked.

He hit the automatic key lock but left the car where it was.

"Let's find the lights and then take a look around the yacht. We'll decide what to do after that."

"Sounds good."

Within minutes Hunter found them and the place was flooded with bright lights.

Flat ramps led up to the vessel and Alex went first, her smooth wedged shoes a great choice for the surface of the deck.

Gingerly she walked along the deck as if she was spying on Marc, but Hunter didn't want to break her concentration. He had no idea what she must be feeling. Marc's deception had deep roots. For him to have blatantly stolen from Alex and then to plan to divorce her was the ultimate slap in the face.

Hunter hoped Marc was in a place where men received no mercy for what he'd done to these three women.

After they'd walked the upper deck, Alex looked back at him. "Ready to go down below?"

"Are you?"

She unbuttoned her short-waist leather jacket and left it on the upper deck. All she wore was a simple lavender T-shirt over jeans. "Yes. It's going to get hot. There's no air-conditioning down there."

Hunter left his jacket too. "I'm going to close and lock the door to the unit. We don't need any visitors."

"I'll wait," she said, sweeping her hair to one side, putting her hand on her hip.

He thought about that naked hip in his hands. How it had responded to his tongue and his voice when he'd told her he needed more of her.

Later. Tonight he'd fulfill his fantasies and hers too.

He got the flashlight from the car and closed the door, locking them inside.

Turning, Alex's head was down, and all he could see was her in profile, thoughtful and distant. They were days away from her being free of Marc. She'd be able to write her own future soon. He wondered if she'd take Jerry's advice and walk away from Wright Enterprises. There were a dozen reasons to leave the company and begin a future free from stress and frustration.

Away from her disrespectful relatives who not only verbally abused her but threatened bodily harm. This was no future for a woman as good as

Alexandria. He just hoped she'd find the incentive to leave.

Hunter headed up the ramp, already feeling the heat of being closed in. "Penny for your thoughts?"

"What else will we find in here?" she asked, her confidence bottoming out.

He tapped her under her chin. "All good things."

"Here goes nothing," she said, and inserted the key.

Walking down the steps, they entered the dining quarters, which were shockingly opulent. Cherrywood glistened as the backdrop of the spacious room that boasted a full galley, regular-size appliances and a dining area with comfortable seating for six. There was a high bar area that served four and a plasma-screen TV built into the wall for viewing pleasure while dining.

"Alex? Come here," Hunter said, heading down a hallway toward a stateroom. "You have to see this."

He opened the drapes as far as they would go. "You have to imagine this on the open sea, but this is amazing. The master suite has two full bathrooms with a private saloon, plasma TV and DVD player."

Alex sat on the bed and put her head in her

hands. "This is amazing. It's gorgeous…and awful. How?" she shook her head. "And Daddy was worried about me buying shoes? This is so much worse." She started laughing.

Hunter came out of the bathroom and looked at her. "Have you completely lost it?"

"I think so. I can't believe it. I've never spent a million dollars on anything. I'm over this. I wish I could just sail away from all of this. I give up. Let's run away and play. Come play with me, Hunter." She laughed.

"No, it's not five o'clock." She was having a sensual meltdown in this overheated boat, yet he didn't find the need to stop her.

She tugged off her shirt. "It's hot, and I want to play with you. We're on a million-dollar boat and it's dark outside."

Hunter laughed. "Sweetheart, this wasn't a million dollars, and I think you're delirious. It's dark because we closed the door."

"You're ruining my sexy mood."

She reached for him and he went to her. She wrapped her arms around his waist as she sat on the bed.

He ran his hands through her hair. "You look punch-drunk."

"Just a little stress that sex can fix."

He caressed her cheek with his thumb. "Tonight. I want to get out of here soon. Let's just make sure there's nothing here and then we can leave. You can sell the boat and put back some of the money. I'd say it's worth at least, I don't know, maybe four hundred thousand."

"We're not even sure there's anything here," she told him as she closed her eyes and rocked him. "Where's the rest of the money? Hmm? Where could it be, Hunter? In here?" She rolled over and opened the drawer on the night table.

He loved the curve of her behind and reached out to strip off her jeans when she pulled a stack of papers out of the drawer. Kicking off her shoes, she folded her legs beneath her and started reading. "Hunter." She patted the bed beside her.

He sat down and looked at the papers in her hand. "They're stock certificates," he said.

"Do these say what I think they say?" she whispered. "That's not Google, is it?"

Hunter could only nod. "Baby, I think your ship just came in."

"How much do you think these are worth?"

Hunter estimated the stack to be about five

inches thick. "Enough to pay back your family and give yourself a nice tip for the rest of your life."

"My name and his name are on them." Alex read them and walked around the stateroom. "This was his insurance policy. If something happened and I found these I would get my money back."

She gestured, shrugged and pulled her fingers through her hair, never saying a word, working out whatever was going on in there.

Finally she stopped and looked at him. "Is this my yacht?" she asked softly.

"Yes. It's yours."

"So I can say 'like new' when I sell it?"

He smiled. "You can. Why?"

She turned her back and looked at him over her shoulder. "Because I want to give it a proper christening by striptease, and then sell it."

She turned around and her jeans were unfastened and so was her bra.

Hunter laughed. "Woman. You're a piece of work."

"You'd better believe it. We're gonna get hotter too. Take this off, Hunter," she said, pulling on his undershirt until he brought it over his head. She wiggled out of her jeans and he saw that she was bare.

He wanted to take her right there, but this was her seduction and he didn't want to rush her.

Alex pushed him back until she was sitting on his lap.

"Your belt is hurting all my tender spots," she said and leaned down, her lips pressed against his.

"Take it off," he said, forcing himself not to ravish her. She tasted so good. His hands swept up the back of her and he couldn't resist wanting to fulfill desires he'd had all day.

His zipper made a jagged sound as it went down and he let her go long enough to get out of his jeans. She was standing on the bed and Hunter captured her breast in his mouth.

"Harder," she urged, her hands caressing him.

Hunter loved the feel of her hair against his skin as it draped him in black luxury.

"Is this where you got shot?"

"Yes."

She licked the scar and kissed it, bringing feeling to a wound that hadn't felt anything in years. Her hands moved over him and stopped on his chest.

"And this?"

"I had open-heart surgery a year ago."

"Oh, sweetheart." She held him against her and rocked him. Her mouth pressed against his, her lips capturing need he didn't know he had. Loneliness he thought he'd gotten over. She reached inside of him and soothed the man in him that needed to be cared for. "Are you better? If you're not, I'm okay with that, too."

She took him down to the bed with her, wrapping her legs around him, her arms and body almost fused to him and his to hers.

"I'm better. I take medicine for it, love. I'll be fine."

He got lost in her gaze.

"Of course you will. You're with me."

He rolled her over and she squealed, laughing. "Where are you taking me?"

"To ecstasy," he said, parting her thighs, seeking the secret folds of her sex. He loved the way she smelled and he loved the way she tasted. Alex moved, her fingers digging into him. "Tell me what you want."

"More, please," she pleaded, scissoring her legs across his back.

Hunter obliged until she came in body-shaking shudders.

He brought her onto his lap and entered her.

"Alex," he groaned.

"Yes?" She sat up straighter, her body moving

in sync with his. She moaned as he gained deeper access. "Mmm?"

"I need more of you."

She hugged him around his neck and he held her tight around her back until he was so deep inside of her he couldn't go any farther. "I'm coming," she cried. "Oh. I love you, Hunter. I love you."

Alex's words undid every caution he'd put in place to guard his head and heart, and he allowed himself to her love.

The hole in his heart closed.

Chapter 16

Alex gripped Hunter's hand and held him back as they stood outside her parents' house, then she kissed him softly. "Maybe I should see my mother by myself. She's kind of shy."

"Alex, I know all about depression. I suffered from it when I was paralyzed, so come on," he said against lips he'd never tire of kissing. "I told her I would visit her. I'm here." He pulled her to him and kissed her again. "We're going to see your mother."

"I hate when you make sense."

"I love your hair."

"I think that's all you love about me, but that's okay, Mr. Smith. I love a challenge." Alex laced her fingers through his and used her key to open the door.

"Mama, it's me. I'm home. Mama! It's Alexandria." They stood in the marble foyer of the grand estate. Hunter was impressed. He'd never seen something so ostentatious, yet so beautiful. There was even a knight positioned behind the grand staircase.

"Lexi. I'm upstairs." The voice had come from an intercom near the front door.

Hunter followed Alex as she ascended the curved staircase leading up to her mother's rooms. Alex opened double French doors and walked inside.

Dorothy Wright lounged on a pink chaise with a magazine, a blanket covering her legs. "Darling, this is an unexpected, joyful surprise."

"Hello, Mother. How are you?"

"Fine now that you're here. Hunter, pleasure to see you again. Tea?"

"No, ma'am, the pleasure is mine. You have a beautiful home."

She smiled as if she didn't believe him. "You only saw the foyer and the stairs. But that's sweet of you."

Dorothy's gaze returned to her daughter. "You sure look pretty. You're glowing."

"I love your hair down, Mama. Where's Daddy?"

"Not here, honey, but we'll save that for another time. What brings you by?"

"Hunter, you want to sit there?" Alex asked, offering him the desk chair.

"No, he doesn't want to be so far away. Bring that over here so you can join us."

Hunter smiled and obeyed. At the desk he saw the familiar stationery that matched the threatening note Alex had received. He wanted to tell her, but there was no good time.

Alex sat at the foot of her mother's chaise. "Mama, I know that you know there's a lot going on at the company. I believe you know that Marc stole a lot of money from Wright Enterprises. What you don't know is that he stole from my personal account as well as from the company. The total came to over $1.1 million."

"I know, and I blame myself."

"Why, Dorothy?" Hunter asked.

"I could have stopped him. I sit here all day with this crippling fear of the outside world. I literally can't leave this house. My marriage is over, and my family is in a state of disrepair because I've not been able to be a good mother."

"Mama, we're grown. Even if you were able to leave the house, there are just some things you can't control."

Dorothy didn't believe her. There was a stubbornness to her jaw. "This I could have stopped. I saw that money disappearing. I watch the accounts online every day. Those large drafts." She put up her finger. "No, Lexi. I wondered what was going on. I could have confronted Marc. Initially I thought they were for land purchases, but there were no contracts to coincide with the purchases. Your father would bring home his briefcase, and I'd go through it with a fine-tooth comb. No deals, no contracts. No log sheets. I knew someone was stealing."

"Confronting him could have gotten you hurt. I'm glad you didn't do that, Dorothy. Marc wasn't known for being violent," Hunter told her, "but he was a pathological liar. He could have easily turned."

"Hunter's right, Mama. So you knew all the theft wasn't coming from Mervyn."

"My son." Dorothy shook her head sadly. "How he breaks my heart. Hunter, I appreciate you. You're saving his life."

"How do you know what happened?"

"My son, ever the resourceful man, called crying for me to get him out of the in-patient facility you graciously had him voluntarily sign himself into."

"To be honest, it wasn't so voluntary."

Dorothy smiled and winked at Hunter. "I know. I told that boy of mine I would help him get out."

"Mama!"

"I would have him arrested at the gate if he didn't sign up for a sixty-day stay. I told him my way. Or my way. He will not threaten to hurt my children. He will not threaten to hurt my child."

Dorothy caressed Alexandria's jaw. "What brings you here, chil'?"

"I found the money that Marc stole and I'm putting it back in the account today, Mama." Alex pulled the check from her pocket and Dorothy clapped her hands to her chest.

"Aren't you just the best woman in the world? I want to be like you when I grow up."

Hunter laughed at Dorothy's happiness.

"Mama, no more notes." Alex looked in her mother's eyes as she said the words.

Dorothy's eyes held the truth. "So, you knew it was me. I guess my scare tactics didn't work so well. I don't want you to suffer. You've got a good thing going with this man, here. Don't ruin it with this company."

"We're taking it one day at a time, Mama. I don't know if I want to run Wright Enterprises. Daddy and Mervyn have stolen my joy in going to work. I feel as if someone is always after me."

"That's no way to feel on your job. What's the worst that can happen if you don't work there? You find your real passion and pursue it, right?" Dorothy said.

"Right," Alex murmured. "But, I'm not sure what that is."

"You're young. You'll find it. Or finish college. Besides, you've got the attention of a very handsome man." Dorothy looked past Alex to Hunter. "Isn't that so?"

"Dorothy, she's the best thing that's happened to me in a long time."

"I like that kind of talk."

Alex took her mother's hand and kissed it. "Mama, can I say one more thing?"

"Yes."

"I want you to get out of this house and see a doctor. Will you, please? I want you to come see my house and spend the night with me and do things with me."

Her mother's face grew a little scared.

"Please, Mama. You deserve love, too. Tell my godfather I said hello."

Knowing flooded her mother's eyes. "He's been wanting me to see a doctor for a long time. It took therapy and his encouragement, and that's how I was able to come to the board meeting."

"Mama, you deserve happiness. Call and tell him you'll see the doctor again."

"I will, darling. Goodbye, Hunter."

Dorothy extended her hand. Hunter kissed her cheek, feeling her love envelop him. This was what he wanted. The love of a family. How could he tell Alex he needed her?

Chapter 17

Alex and Hunter emerged from the fifteenth-floor elevator the same time as Danielle and Tristan exited the elevator across from them. Despite their rocky past, Alex ran over to Danielle with her arms wide.

"Hello, wife-in-law. Can a sista get a hug?"

Danielle shook her head, smiling. "You're still you."

"Who else would I be? Hug me."

Danielle hugged Alex for a good long while then stepped back. Bygones were bygones.

"You look good," Danielle told her. "You been okay?"

Alex wiped her curls back. "It's been a struggle, but I'm getting there. This thing with Marc has taken me through a lot of changes."

"For you too?" Danielle stepped back on one booted foot and shook her head. "From the grave he's still messing with me. Where's Renee?"

The elevator bell rang and the doors opened. Renee emerged with Chris at her side. "Hey," she said, and Alex and Danielle rushed to her side.

The three hugged. Danielle broke apart first and opened her purse. "Are either of you going to need a tissue?"

Alex had been emotional all week. Her meltdown on the yacht and their passionate love-making made Hunter wonder if a simple piece of cotton could contain all that was inside her.

He loved that about her. She wasn't afraid to express emotion anymore, but he'd been keeping a secret from her and Alex had been facing all her demons and defeating them. He wondered if he should tell her the truth about Marc.

"I don't need tissue," Alex said, "You, Renee?"

"No."

Let's go then," Alex said softly.

"Tristan?" Danielle reached her hand out to him and he took it and kissed the back.

Alex didn't call his name, she just looked at him. She let the others pass and waited for him, then put her arm around his waist.

"You're going to be fine," Hunter told her.

"Okay."

"No matter the results."

"That's right, because he's dead."

Renee and Danielle started laughing, but stopped as they proceeded into the law office reception area. Chris announced their arrival and everyone grew quiet.

The somber-faced receptionist escorted them to a conference room where they waited.

Alex tried to be still, but Hunter could feel her nervousness. He reached for her hand and held it under the table.

"Where's your dog?" Tristan asked.

"Little Sweetie has a play date with my assistant's dog. So he's been gone this past week."

"I thought you couldn't manage without him," Danielle said with curious eyes.

"We've been very busy." Alex looked at Hunter. "Haven't we?"

"Yes. The attorneys should be in any minute now."

Hunter knew Danielle was fishing, but what Alex decided to divulge was her business. She wasn't saying much and he appreciated her discretion, although after she'd told him she loved him, he felt like telling the world.

He knew that feeling would pass. Soon Alex wasn't going to need him. She'd go back to her normal life and he'd return to his.

Maybe he'd get to play his saxophone. Since starting this job for Chris, he hadn't had time to practice. But this had become so much more than a job; he'd found the woman he wanted to be with. But she could be attached to a dead man that could screw with her life for a long time.

What kind of toll would that take on their relationship?

She'd paid back the money, but would her family continue to be a pain in the behind? Would Alex keep letting them abuse her?

Hunter knew he wouldn't allow it if she were his woman.

Two attorneys walked, a man and woman, the man reminding him of a black Santa Claus. Stout, he walked around and shook each of their hands. "I'm Attorney Leonard Moore. How do you do?"

Everyone smiled as they shook his hand, and there was an immediate likability to him. His counterpart wasn't as affable, and sat down once Leonard returned to the head of the table.

"This is my legal assistant, Marla Montana. From my understanding we're here to determine who is the legal Mrs. Marc Foster. Is that correct?"

"Yes," the three ladies chimed together.

Leonard smiled. "May I ask in what way this information will be used?"

The ladies look at one another.

"Can you explain your question?" Alex asked.

"Are you planning litigation against one other?"

"No," all spoke again.

"Okay," Leonard said after no one offered any additional explanation. "Let's get down to business. Mrs. Danielle Timmons-Foster married Marc Foster five years ago in Atlanta in a small ceremony by Judge Carlton Hoyt. Is that correct?"

Danielle nodded. "That's correct."

"That union was paid for by check by Mr. Marc Foster in the amount of thirty dollars."

"Correct," Danielle agreed.

Leonard nodded.

"Mrs. Renee Mitchell-Foster. You married Marc Foster two years ago in Opelika, Alabama, is that correct?"

"Yes, that's correct."

"He paid for that marriage as well, but by credit card in the amount of sixty-five dollars, and the marriage certificate was signed by both parties, correct?"

"Yes, I made sure of that, as well as by the judge and the witness."

"Very good," Leonard commented, and made a check mark on his notes.

"Mrs. Alexandria Lord Wright-Foster, you were married in the Bahamas, is that correct?" Leonard asked.

"Yes."

"Marc Foster paid for the marriage certificate and license?"

"No, I did."

Leonard looked up. "I see. Then what happened?"

"I gave the paperwork to Marc. He was supposed to sign and give them to the judge."

Leonard sighed. He drew his mouth together and nodded for a moment.

"Ladies, you know we are dealing with the

actions of a confidence man. A man who conned you for one reason or another. I don't know why. There's no explanation. But before I give you this news, I want to tell you what has been done right.

"You're not fighting each other. You're not bitter, and the best thing of all is that you're healing. Be happy with your lives and new loves. Now to the results. Marla."

She stood with a box of tissue in her hand.

"Danielle Timmons-Foster, Marc Foster bounced the check for your marriage certificate. He was informed of this before the wedding and he issued another check before the proceedings.

"You two were married and it was found out afterward that the second check was also insufficient. As a result of those findings, your marriage certificate was issued but the certificate you were supposed to receive by mail with the official seal was never mailed. Therefore, I'm sorry to say, your marriage is invalid."

"You're kidding," Danielle said. "Let me see the marriage certificate."

Marla passed the certificate to Danielle, who ran her fingers over every inch of it. "It's not there."

"No, ma'am," Leonard said.

Alex squeezed Hunter's hand. He rubbed it to still her nervousness in the face of Danielle's news.

"I'm sorry," Leonard said. "Would you like to take a moment?"

No one moved. Tristan finally leaned close to Danielle and whispered something. Then, "No," he said. "Let's proceed."

"Alexandria Lord Wright-Foster, Marc Foster married you in the Bahamas. You admittedly gave the documents to Mr. Foster to sign. He never gave them to the judge. He forged the judge's signature, but he, Marc, didn't sign them himself. His name is forged on your document."

"Wait a second. Marc forged the judge's name, and had someone else sign his name?" Alex asked.

"Yes."

"Okay. Thank you." Sweeping her hair over her shoulder, she squeezed Hunter's hand for reassurance.

"Mrs. Renee Mitchell-Foster. Your documents are the only ones that have been authenticated, and I believe that's only because of your diligence. You are the legal Mrs. Marc Jacob Foster."

"Thank you," Renee said, looking as if she'd won a bathtub full of rattlesnakes.

"He said he wanted to have children," Danielle said, her hand on her chest.

"Marc was infertile, Danielle. He couldn't have children," Chris said into the silence.

Marla set a glass of water in front of Danielle and put the box of tissue on the table.

"I wasted five years of my life," Danielle said brokenly and inhaled sharply. "I can't believe it."

"Baby, don't cry," Tristan said.

Alex hurried around the table and put her arms around Danielle. "Okay, okay," Alex said as wracking sobs tore from the usually composed woman. "I'm so sorry. I'm sorry. It's over. It's over. I'm so sorry."

Renee came over too, and held her. "Danielle, he wasn't a prize. Really, if I could give him away I would."

"You can still have children," Alex told her. "You can still fall in love and have a happy life. You're so pretty. Please don't cry. Really, Renee's worse off than us, Danielle."

Hunter loved that she was still searching for a way to make them all happy.

Danielle looked at her. "Why?"

"I'm married to a pathological, lying, dead felon." Renee reached for the box of tissue Marla had put on the table and dabbed her eyes.

"That's awful," Danielle said. She stood up and hugged Renee and Alex. "I'm sorry, Renee."

Hunter looked at Tristan and Chris. "They're strange ladies."

"They're working it out," Tristan told.

"They're amazing," Chris said.

Renee's nose had turned red. "Danielle, do you want to play in Alex's makeup?"

She chuckled. "You two are so funny. Thank you, but I think I have some."

"We like being your wives-in-law," Alex told her. "Don't cry for him. Otherwise you wouldn't have met us."

"I'm not crying for him. Just the time I wasted. The dreams I falsely invested in," Danielle said, looking at Tristan.

"From here on we're making new dreams," Renee told her.

"Hunter, pass me my purse, please?" Alex dug inside and pulled out her checkbook. "How much is today's meeting, Leonard?"

"The bill is being paid by Chris Foster." Leonard went and stood with the men while Marla had joined the women.

"Chris, please allow me to handle this," Alex said.

"No," Chris said. "My brother did you all

wrong. I couldn't have stopped him, but I can at least make things a little easier."

"No," the three wives insisted.

"Chris, you're not responsible for Marc's sins. We're going to be okay from this point forward. Might take some time, but we'll get better," Danielle told him as she pulled out her checkbook too. "Leonard, how much is it?"

"Forty-five hundred dollars."

Renee wrote her check slower. "Deposit this Monday. Hey, mine will have to come from my next paycheck."

Alex put her hand on Renee's. "Please. I'll take care of yours. You can pick up my dinner check, and I'll tell you about the depth of your husband's deceit."

Chapter 18

The newly hired captain of the *Marc III* cut through the waters of Lake Allatoona at a leisurely pace as the three couples stood above deck enjoying the evening sun.

"How did he buy this yacht without you knowing, Alex?" Chris asked.

"He embezzled money from my family's company and he stole from our personal account. He forged my signature on checks just like he forged the judge's name on our marriage certificate."

"He had this yacht renovated and had plans to

sell it. We found evidence in a cabinet above Alex's refrigerator," Hunter added.

Danielle shook her head in disbelief. "I've been through my house fifteen times, and I've looked in every drawer and shoe box, and never considered looking in that tiny cabinet. How'd you even think to look there?"

A healthy breeze tossed Danielle's hair into the air and Alex clapped. "Good gracious, you're gorgeous!" Everyone laughed. "In all seriousness, Hunter figured it out," Alex said.

"Alex's brother planted the seed. He said that Marc was always in the kitchen cooking, ordering spices off the Internet. The cabinet is above the refrigerator. Alex can't reach it. Even if she stood on a chair."

"It makes sense, Dani," Tristan said. "We'll check it when we get back to your place."

"Okay."

Alex watched the couple, hoping that something would develop. Danielle still looked as if she'd been a witness to a horrible crime, but Alex knew that would go away with time.

"Alex admitted that she'd never used the cabinet. It was a perfect hiding place. We gambled that Marc would get sloppy and he did," Hunter finished.

"You two are amazing detectives," Renee said, pushing up her brand-new sunglasses. "What will you do now?"

"Sell the yacht," Alex told her. "I've already taken care of my family. There were some other issues going on as well. I'm not sure I'm the best person to run the company. I don't want to be the problem though. In the next couple weeks, I'll decide if I should stay on."

"Wow. You sound so mature," Danielle told her. "I'm impressed."

"I knew you liked me! Give me a hug." Alex embraced Danielle, who pretended to cringe.

"What will you do if you quit?" Tristan asked.

"I don't know. Hunter might need a spy for his company. Right, sweetheart?"

Alex knew she was putting him on the spot, but he hadn't said one word to her since they'd split up from the attorney's office.

She'd invited everyone to dinner on the yacht and Hunter hadn't objected. So the ladies had decided to go shopping for swimsuits and the guys for food.

Hunter had agreed to take care of hiring the captain for the evening. She'd given him her credit card and took off with the girls, agreeing to meet them at the marina at seven.

He hadn't said a word, not even about the swim trunks and T-shirt she'd bought him.

"I think I've got enough spies," he finally said.

"Aw, and I was just sharpening my skills. Oh, well. Maybe something else." She played off his rejection and pulled a bottle of wine from the built-in bucket. "Anybody for more wine before I go below to check on dinner?"

"I'll check on it with you," Renee said.

"Why don't I take over wine duty," Chris offered. "I don't want dinner to burn. It smells delicious."

"Thank you," she said, proud that she'd been able to make some of them happy.

Renee followed Alex down into the galley and pulled out the salad fixings. After washing her hands, she started tearing lettuce and cutting vegetables, arranging them into the most beautiful salad Alex and ever seen. Danielle joined them and buttered garlic bread to pop in at the last second.

"Hunter's feelings are hurt, Alex," Renee told her.

"Why?" Alex looked between the girls. "What happened?"

"I don't know why. Maybe because he doesn't have a reason to hang around you anymore," Renee told her.

"From the time you arrived in California I could tell he wanted you," Danielle said.

"I want him too. But he doesn't want someone to need him. He told me that weeks ago, and I need a man to need me. You know what I mean?"

Renee stopped chopping and Danielle stopped buttering to look at her. "What?"

"I need a man to need me. To want to be around me. To want to be in my space, in my life. Hunter's been there for me. Every step of the way. But Chris hired him. Then I hired him."

"That's different. I see the way he looks at you. He doesn't want to let you go," Danielle said. "He was looking at you like that in California, just a little, but now…a lot."

"The thing is, girls," Alex said, preparing the pasta, "I'm afraid of making another mistake. Marc and I weren't in love in the end. I want real love."

The door to the galley opened and Hunter walked in, his shirt wet, Chris behind him, looking apologetic.

"You guys having a wet T-shirt contest without us?" Alex asked him. She wanted to hug him so bad, she ached. He stood in the doorway looking uncomfortable.

"Chris decided I should get a little wet. Did you get me another shirt?"

"No, just one. It didn't occur to me that you'd need another. I have another bikini top." She giggled, hoping he would laugh, but he didn't. He headed toward their stateroom. She looked at the girls and they encouraged her to follow him.

Alex followed him, her head down. She walked inside, shut and locked the door. She pulled the strings on her top and tossed it to him.

"What are you doing?" he asked.

"Giving you the shirt off my back. It's a bikini, but you get the meaning."

He picked up the flowered top and fingered it.

Alex lay on the bed and patted the space next to her. "What?" he said.

"I've upset you. Lie down and talk to me. What happened?"

"Alex, you gave me your credit card."

"I'm sorry."

"That was the first time I felt like you hired me to do a job for you."

Her eyes burned at the thought that she might lose him. "I didn't mean it like that. I didn't want you to have to pay for the captain. I was thinking I'm getting rid of this boat that reminds me of

Marc and what he put me through, and I didn't want you to pay for that. I didn't want you to see it a month from now on your credit card statement and think about him again.

"I'm sorry. I didn't mean to offend you. Will you lie down with me now?"

She covered her nipples as he lay on his side next to her.

"What are you doing?"

"You arouse me. You make me feel like a desirable and protected and cared-for woman. But you scare me, too."

"What? Why?"

"You told me all the things you don't want in a woman." She felt herself beginning to cry and she took a deep breath. "You told me all the things you didn't want. But never what you wanted. I don't know if I even have a chance to win your heart."

"Alex, if you only knew how much you've healed me."

"Tell me." She inched closer.

He put his hand on her hip. "You fill me up. I love your energy and enthusiasm. Your optimism and vitality. You're so compassionate and caring. I saw you with Danielle today and if I wasn't already in love with you, I would have fallen in love with you right then. With your mother at the meeting a few weeks ago. When you thought she'd given the company to Mervyn. You didn't turn against her."

He kissed her lips. "You were so kind to her. And then this morning you were so gentle with her. I can't imagine my life without you. I don't want you to be a spy for me. I want you to be a wife to me. I want to be a husband to you. You're funny and happy and optimistic. I support you going to school, but you have to love yourself, Alex. Because I love you, Alex."

Her heart sang with joy.

"I love you too. I thought I scared you the other night."

He nodded. "I was afraid that I'd told you a lot of things that I wouldn't be able to take back. I need you. I want you. I want you in my life forever. But I have a question."

"What is it?"

"What if I found a piece of paper that said something about Marc not wanting to be with you anymore? Would you want to see it?"

"No, I couldn't care less. The man I want is lying next to me right now."

She inched closer and slipped her hand

beneath his damp T-shirt. Hunter lifted and pulled it off.

She kissed his scars and hugged him hard.

"Harder," he said, holding her too.

"I'm going to love you forever, Hunter."

Hunter couldn't resist kissing the woman he vowed to love forever. "This time it's for good."

* * * * *

Kimani Romance is excited to present
The next explosive episode of
THE THREE MRS. FOSTERS miniseries,
Featuring three scintillating titles
by three nationally bestselling authors!

Don't miss Renee Foster's story
THE PERFECT MAN *by Carla Fredd...*
Before Renee Foster can forget her past,
she needs her ex-brother-in-law's help.
Renee needs FBI agent Chris Foster to get to
the bottom of his late brother's double-dealing,
three-time-marrying and larcenous deceptions.
But as she works with Chris to uncover the
truth, Renee soon realizes that Chris is unlike
other men. He's not intimidated by her intelligence,
and he sees past her aloof manner to the home-
loving, passionate person she truly is...

Every marriage has a secret—or three...

THE PERFECT MAN
by Carla Fredd
Kimani Romance #93
On sale June 2008

USA TODAY BESTSELLING AUTHOR

BRENDA JACKSON

IRRESISTIBLE FORCES

Taylor Steele wants a baby, not a relationship. So she
proposes a week of mind-blowing sex in the Caribbean
to tycoon Dominic Saxon, whose genes seem perfect.
No strings—just mutual enjoyment. But when it's over,
will either of them be able to say goodbye?

"Brenda Jackson has written another sensational novel...
stormy, sensual and sexy—all the things a romance reader
could want in a love story."
—*Romantic Times BOOKreviews* on *Whispered Promises*

*Coming the first week of May
wherever books are sold.*

KIMANI™
ROMANCE

www.kimanipress.com

KPBJ0640508

Down and out...but not really

Indiscriminate Attraction

ESSENCE BESTSELLING AUTHOR
Linda Hudson-Smith

Searching the streets and homeless shelters for his missing
twin, shabbily disguised Chad Kingston accepts volunteer
Laylah Versailles's help. Luscious Laylah's determination
to turn "down-and-out" Chad's life around has a heated
effect on him. But Chad's never trusted women—
and Laylah has secrets.

"Hudson-Smith does an outstanding job...
A truly inspiring novel!"
—*Romantic Times BOOKreviews* on *Secrets & Silence*

*Coming the first week of May
wherever books are sold.*

KIMANI™
ROMANCE

www.kimanipress.com   KPLHS0660508

her kind of *Man*

Favorite author
PAMELA YAYE

As a gawky teen, Makayla Stevens yearned for
Kenyon Blake. Now he's the uncle of one of her students,
and wants to get better acquainted with Makayla.
The reality is even hotter than her teenage fantasies.
But their involvement could damage her career…
and her peace of mind.

"*Other People's Business*…is a fun and lighthearted story…
an entertaining novel."
—*Romantic Times BOOKreviews* on
Pamela Yaye's debut novel

*Coming the first week of May
wherever books are sold.*

KIMANI
ROMANCE

www.kimanipress.com   KPPY0670508

"Byrd proves once again that she's
a wonderful storyteller."
—*Romantic Times BOOKreviews*
on *The Beautiful Ones*

ACCLAIMED AUTHOR

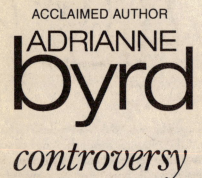

ADRIANNE byrd

controversy

Michael Adams is no murderer—even if she did
joke about killing her ex-husband after their nasty
divorce. Now she has to prove to investigating
detective Kyson Dekker that she's innocent.
Of course, it doesn't help that he's so distractingly
gorgeous that Michael can't think straight....

**Coming the first week of May
wherever books are sold.**

ARABESQUE®

www.kimanipress.com   KPABI000508

Her dreams of love came true...twice.

ESSENCE BESTSELLING AUTHOR

DONNA HILL

Charade

Betrayed by Miles Bennett, the first man she'd let into her heart, Tyler Ellington flees to Savannah where she falls for photographer Sterling Grey. Sterling is everything Miles is not...humorous, compassionate, honest. But when she returns to New York, Tyler is yet again swayed by Miles's apologies and passion. Now torn between two men, she must decide which love is the real thing.

"A lighthearted comedy, rich in flavor and unpredictable in story, *Divas, Inc.* proves how limitless this author's talent is."
—*Romantic Times BOOKreviews*

Coming the first week of May wherever books are sold.

ARABESQUE®

www.kimanipress.com

KPDHI010508

*Overcoming the past to enjoy
the present can be difficult...*

YOLONDA TONETTE SANDERS

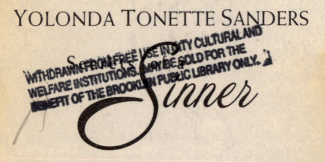

Sinner

After years of doing whatever was necessary to survive,
Natalie Coleman finally feels her life is getting back on
track. Returning to the home she ran from years ago, she
confronts the painful events of her past. As old wounds
heal, Natalie realizes God has led her home to show her
that every sinner can be saved, every life redeemed.

"Need a little good news in your novels? Look no further."
—*Essence* on *Soul Matters*

Coming the first week of May wherever books are sold.